They gazed at each other for a long time while Eloise battled a fiery desire to press her mouth against Marian's. Suddenly, Marian put her hand on the back of Eloise's head and drew her lips to her own. Her kiss was gentle, warm, inviting. Eloise experienced the sensation of balmy water washing over her body.

Then they separated, their hands resting upon each other's arms. Marian led them through the front door. Hand-in-hand, they stood at the threshold of the house. There was enough moonlight so that Eloise could see the highlights in Marian's eyes. A ripple somewhat like a small electric current passed upward through her fingertips and into her arms, fading somewhere within the center of her chest. The jolt seemed to emanate from their clasped hands.

Marian's voice trembled as she whispered, "I feel strange . . . light-headed. Holy, almost. The ground," she said, looking down, "feels sacred. The soil beneath my feet . . ." Her voice trailed off into inaudible words.

Yes, that was how Eloise was feeling, as though together they had entered a paradisiacal retreat. A deep spiritual fulfillment touched her. "I must see you—often, Marian. I . . . must. I . . . can't explain it." Marian listened without moving. Eloise pushed on, not comprehending her own words. "I don't think I'll be a complete person if I don't. I'll be lost." She tossed back her head and looked at the stars, frustrated, pleading for understanding, not from Marian, but from something higher up, something more profound.

Visit

Bella Books

at

BellaBooks.com

or call our toll-free number

1-800-729-4992

The Tomstown Incident

▼

Penny Hayes

Bella
BOOKS

2004

Bella Books, Inc.
P.O. Box 10543
Tallahassee, FL 32302

Printed in the United States of America on acid-free paper
First Edition

Editor: Christi Cassidy
Cover designer: Sandy Knowles

ISBN 1-931513-56-2

To Joyce, the one I love.

Author's Note:

There is no Tomstown. General Herkimer is real. All other characters are fictitious. The location of the story is generally accurate as is General Herkimer's march.

Prologue
1946

Diary entry, May 6th, 1915

Today I am full of silly thoughts.

I wonder if anyone other than I have ever asked the question: Is the one I was intended to love not of this time? Has he already been born? Lived an entire life? Or is he presently so completely, so deeply, so powerfully in love that there is no question, nay, would the question even arise as to whether the one loved is or is not his kindred soul mate? But for the rest of us, we who seemingly already care equally as much for another, must we, with clandestine and shameful thoughts, ask: Is this person, lying so peacefully warm beside me this night as he has a thousand other nights, not really my incarnate soul mate?

Why such a question if, in my present circumstance, I believe I'm living in complete happiness? Why would such a thought even arise? Do others ask: *Was I born too late? Too early? Knowing that this time in which I presently exist, does not feel quite comfortable?*

There abides within me a sense of unbalance, of longing and loneliness, and I cannot quite put my finger on it. I am struck as though bludgeoned by a heavy, leaden hammer in the bosom of my breast, feeling that a dreadful burden of pining by someone cries out to me as I can presently now feel myself crying out to him with equal zeal. The sensation is quite magnetic as I gaze across time, fighting to conjure up his image, to put form and substance to his body, to bring light to his eyes.

Perchance I fail at this unrealistic task because the person I seek no longer exists, not even as a tiny speck of dust so long has he laid "a-moldering" in his grave, and what remains in his stead is his lonely soul lamenting with the same sense of longing and belief that he too missed out on his heart's destiny by being born too soon. Perhaps only our own two souls have a complete understanding of each other's need, that is, to join together to be truly at rest and peace, and until that moment both will experience agony as only souls can, and that complete peace cannot happen until both living beings are joined together in life—or both are dead. If this be the case, then I shall soon know.

Mary Scott Greenfield

ELOISE

"Eloise, dear," Eloise's grandmother called from the foot of the attic stairs, her voice high and clear, reminding Eloise of birds when they first begin to sing each morning. "Come on down out of there, now. The rain's quit, and the ground's dried off. You can go outside and play."

Eloise Scott-Greenfield Webster (the hyphenated middle name given in keeping with the family tradition of each grandchild carrying at least two prior surnames so that no one from the past would be forgotten), looked upward toward the west end of the high-peaked attic roof. A four-paned window, set at a forty-five-degree angle at the apex of the house, revealed a sunny day. Eloise's heart raced as she rammed the thin, leather-jacketed journal deep beneath ancient clothing, old shoes, wide-brimmed flowered hats, and photo albums crammed full of faded, tatter-edged pictures, yellowed newspaper clippings, turn-of-the-century postcards and letters. There were hanks of hair tied with pieces of faded ribbon and stored in individual envelopes with names neatly written in Palmer penmanship. Grandma's big old leather trunk reeked of mildew and mothballs.

She slammed the lid shut; dust flew upward into her face and danced in long, playful sunbeams stretching from the window to where she hurriedly put things aright.

She sneezed several times as she thought of Grandma's book. There were too many big words in it for her. She was only in the fourth grade. Well, in September she would be. Besides, Eloise Scott-Greenfield Webster suspected Grandma would skin her alive if she was ever caught reading that dusty old diary. Everybody knew what a diary was—private!

She skirted several more packing trunks, assorted sizes of cardboard boxes, old rugs, discarded furniture and lamps while ducking beneath outdated suits and dresses tiredly hanging overhead on fraying clotheslines strung from beam to beam. Racing pell-mell, she bounded down the dark, narrow staircase, zipped through her grandparents' bedroom, exited downstairs by way of the bannister, scooted through the living room and into the kitchen. Panting, she slid to an abrupt halt before her grandmother who sat on a blue plastic-upholstered, chrome-legged chair beside a white Formica-topped table scarred with scratches and cuts from years of cooking for her husband and now widely dispersed four grown children. The table was covered with scraps of cloth, plain blue linen and dull white.

Last night while Eloise slept, Grandma had stayed up and sewed. Her sewing ability was legendary. To prove it she had stacks of first-place blue ribbons from several county fairs stuffed in boxes and drawers here and there. She bragged that she could knock out blouses, skirts and dresses in record time on that old Minnesota treadle machine, but zippered flies in pants drove her crazy. Eloise's mother had often mentioned Grandma's skills and always marveled that anyone could sew so fast, often without using a pattern and always without electricity. "Don't need it, don't want it," Grandma told everybody. "Treadle does me just fine," she said, using the name she had long ago given to her precious sewing machine.

Grandma Mary Scott Greenfield, aged fifty-three, with nary a wrinkle in her tanned face other than a few crows' feet radiating off each side of her chocolate-brown eyes and deep smile lines extending from her nostrils to each side of her narrow lips, ran slightly on the plump side. Beneath a printed cotton bib-apron she wore her customary flowered summer dress, a simple design that slipped over her head, buttoned loosely at the neck and tied with a bow in the back to take up excess cloth at the waist. Eloise once counted six such dresses in Grandma's closet, each with a different flowered print.

"See here, Eloise. I've got something for you."

Eloise knew Grandma had been working on something important. They had eaten supper in the living room last night to spare her having to clear the table before her project was completed. Eloise was not the least interested in sewing and hadn't bothered to see what Grandma was making. Now, she looked, wide-eyed and stunned.

Her mouth opened and closed, opened and closed again before she could speak. "For me?" she whispered, taking the clothing in her hands. Her grandmother had made a skirt of blue linen and a blouse of white cotton. The skirt was gathered at the waist with a drawstring to hold it in place. The blouse was plain with long sleeves gathered at the wrists and a small collar at the neck. She looked at Grandma.

"For you, Eloise." Grandma smiled. "You know. Like the little girls in days of old. Here, now, shimmy out of those clothes and put these on. Let's see how they fit."

Two minutes later, Eloise looked like she belonged in the eighteenth century. Her body trembled with joy as she ran her hands down the front of the blouse and then over her hips. "They fit perfect, Grandma. Just perfect. It feels so nice."

"Stand still, child. I can't tie this bow when you're fidgeting so."

Eloise Webster—wiry, wafer-thin, eyes as blue as today's fresh noon sky, her grandma always said, and too large for her narrow,

5

tanned face—yearned only to run, to be free beneath the sun and clad in her beautiful new "old" clothes. Grandma had made them especially for her alone.

"Oh, I love them, Grandma, and I love you."

Grandma and Grandpa had another daughter, Heather, besides Eloise's mother, Betty, and two sons, Charles and Walter. Eloise loved her aunts and uncles, but as much as she loved them, and Grandpa, too, she still loved Grandma the best. Her grandparents seldom saw their other children since they now all lived in distant states having one by one, as they married, left New York. They now came home only for Thanksgiving, Christmas and sometimes for their parents' birthdays. Mommy, Daddy and she lived in Binghamton, not too long a drive to Frankfort Center where her grandparents' lived. As a result, her relatives' paths rarely crossed hers.

Again, Eloise's hands caressed the fabric while her grandmother continued fussing over her. "Please hurry, Grandma," she whined. Instantly contrite, she froze, tightening her hands into small fists, fighting to control her energy. Visiting Grandma and Grandpa without her parents along for the first time ever, she felt terribly grown up, but she wasn't behaving that way right now. "I'm sorry, Grandma." She was scheduled for a two-week visit. Another rude reaction like that could shorten her stay by a week and five days.

Grandma heaved a dramatic sigh. "I understand, dear. I was once a fidgeter myself. Still am, according to your grandpa."

She adjusted the skirt's waist one more time while Eloise closed her eyes and bit her lower lip to avoid tearing herself away from her grandmother's small, fussing hands.

"Now," Grandma said, "stand back and let me take a good look at you. Yes," she said with a critical eye. "This'll do you just fine. Hmm." Her hand went to her chin and thoughtfully rubbed it.

"Grandma!" Eloise whispered, barely able to contain herself. Her very insides itched to run; to fly! She tightened her buttocks and calf muscles, an almost involuntary act she often utilized when trapped in a situation from which she could not readily escape. Sunday services was one of those times. Hot, spring days during the tail end of the school year was another, and this prolonged fussing by Grandma was the worst yet.

"All right, Eloise. Go on, and watch where you step. Don't forget you're barefoot."

Indeed she was barefoot; she had been shoeless just as soon as her parents had driven out of sight and would stay that way until her visit with her grandparents had ended. Now she barely heard the last of Grandma's warnings as she bolted through the back screen door of the kitchen, swinging it wide open on squeaking hinges. She burst free out into the welcoming hot July sun. The door slammed against the big house's old white clapboard siding, knocking off a few more aging, curling chips of white paint as she sailed over the three wooden steps leading from porch to ground. Puffs of dust exploded beneath her rapid steps as her feet struck the earth, and her long, honey-colored braids flew out behind her. She aimed for the right side of the old, two-story barn once proudly housing horses, carriages, chickens and pigs, but now off limits to her because of its dangerously deteriorating condition. She would get a good scolding if she went inside where now scrap lumber and tools lay scattered about.

Behind the barn, a large meadow of knee-high grass awaited her. At the field's farthest edge grew a sizable forest of hardwood trees, their trunks expansive from age. Some of them were "'bout as old as time," Grandpa had told her. Virgin timber, he called them. They were still standing, he said, "'cause somebody had sense enough not to cut down every danged tree in New York State." The trees were so tall she had to crane her neck to see their tops. From time to time somebody offered to cut them down for a good price. Grandpa always said no. "Let's not destroy the rest of what's left of America," Eloise had heard him say more than once over the years. She hadn't understood his words at the time.

A bubbly, cold stream meandered through the woods where she and Grandma were going picnicking one day soon. Once when she

7

and her parents had come to visit and she was still a very little girl, she thought she saw a town out there, but babies had powerful imaginations and saw lots of stuff that wasn't really there, and she was no longer a baby, and she never saw the town again.

She tore around the back of the barn, pausing at the edge of the field, listening. Grandpa was over in the woods by the stream this morning, clearing away some of the scrub trees so that others might grow larger and faster. The rhythmic chopping of his razor-sharp axe striking wood told her that she wouldn't be allowed near there today, not without Grandma by her side.

Having reached her destination, it was no longer so important to run. She breathed deeply of the early-summer odors and felt far removed from modern day. She was properly dressed and ready to get on the first wagon that rolled by. It would be drawn by a team of stout, brown horses or maybe oxen. She'd sit high on the seat and drive the team herself.

She heard a car drive by out front of the house. It broke her spell. But not for long. She was here, again, letting her gaze drift across the field. Soft breezes caused the grass to undulate like freshly laundered sheets gently rippling on Grandma's clothesline.

Something was poking the bottom of her left foot. She stepped aside to see what it was. The grass being too deep she had to bend over and pull it aside. She found a strange-looking rusty old nail. She picked it up and studied it. The nail looked nothing like any she'd ever seen; approximately three inches long, it was badly rusted, a trifle bent and strangely square on all four sides. She stuffed the curiosity in her apron pocket. Later today, she would ask Grandpa about it.

Her nose twitched and a smile crossed her face. The faint aroma of baking bread whiffed through the air. Gosh, did Grandma already have bread in the oven? That was fast! Her heart exploded with joy. It was going to be a perfect day.

The aroma became stronger as she stood at the grassland's edge. To her surprise, three girls about her own age were playing in the middle of the field. She wondered who they were and how she had missed them yesterday when she had first ventured alone into the meadow after her parents had left. Like her, the girls were barefoot and hatless, but each wore a simple tan dress, loose and comfortable, and over that, a bib-apron like her own and Grandma's.

Also surprising, in the distance stood the town off to her right, the very one that she thought she had once spotted years ago. She blinked several times, but the village stayed put. Confusion creased her brow as she studied the small hamlet. There were no cars or trucks, but there were horses and buggies. The houses were built mainly of stone, a few stood two stories high, and many were surrounded by white picket fences. A backhouse stood several yards behind every house. Wisps of smoke rose lazily upward from the chimneys. A single main street of rutted dirt ran through town. People were out wandering around or working in back yards. Several lines of laundry were hanging out to dry. How could she have not seen this place every time she'd ever been here?

More curious about the children than the strange town, she put aside her puzzling thoughts and watched the girls as they whacked at wooden hoops with sticks, trying to make them roll through the grass.

Slowly she made her way toward them. The bigger girl was exceptionally skilled at rolling her band using only a thin, sturdy stick to keep it upright and moving forward. The others were having more trouble, taking turns with one stick and sharing a single hoop that often tipped and fell. "You'll get it if you keep trying," the better player of the three encouraged. "You've almost got it now."

Eloise paused, waited to be noticed. The smallest child spotted her, letting the wobbling hoop roll to a shaky stop before toppling over. Eloise raised her hand and shyly waved.

"Hi," she called. A big grin split her face. They were now all watching her. She'd been wondering if there were other kids around here. Now she'd have playmates during her two-week visit.

With smiles equal to hers, the girls gathered their hoops and walked over to her. "Good morning," said the taller girl. "And are you new moved here?"

Eloise shrugged. "I'm visiting my grandma and grandpa for a couple of weeks. My name's Eloise. What's yours?"

The taller girl answered, "I'm Marian Jones, and this is my little sister, Agnes, and this here's our friend, Nancy Jane Helm."

Marian was Eloise's height, exactly four feet, two inches. She was a lean but strong-looking child. Her eyes were light brown, her skin a sun-rich tan. Flaxen hair flowed freely down her back; the sun-bleached eyebrows set off her merry eyes. When she smiled she revealed teeth that were fine and white, with the exception of a slightly awry front tooth and a canine going bad on the left. She had a deep dimple in her chin much like Grandpa's, but softer-looking. A cleft, he'd called it. SA valley, she'd tease, his was so deep.

Agnes and Nancy Jane were both nearly four feet tall. Agnes' eyes and hair were the color of her sister's, while Nancy Jane's eyes were hazel, speckled with tiny golden flecks, and her hair a flaming red. The other girls' teeth were in better shape than Marian's, even though Nancy Jane was missing two in front. The younger girls wore their tresses in long braids down their backs.

"Where'd you get the hoops?" Eloise asked. "Can I roll it?"

Immediately, Marian offered hers. "Here," she said. "Just give it a good roll and strike the stick across the top of it like this." She gave a short demonstration and then handed the stick and hoop to Eloise.

Eloise tried it several times and found it wasn't as easy a task as it looked.

"I'm not good at all," Nancy Jane said.

"You're better than me," Eloise said. "I can't keep it going at all." She tried until all four girls fell to the earth squealing in a fit of giggles. The hoop had continued to defeat her.

"I want to try it again," screeched Agnes. The hoops passed between the four of them as they took turns, with Marian calling out suggestions. Before long, the four of them were screaming with laughter and holding their aching sides.

A loud, high-pitched, no-nonsense voice called out to them from the edge of the field, "Girls, where are you?"

Eloise's new friends froze and looked toward the village. "Mama!" Agnes whispered.

Marian glanced at the morning sun. "We'll be scolded and not have supper today, I think." Her eyes filled with worry. "We should have milked the cow by now."

"And fed the chickens." Agnes, too, seemed frightened.

"You were supposed to keep watch," Marian hissed. "Everybody in Tomstown will hear her ahollerin'."

Nancy Jane said nothing, obviously picking up on the fear of the sisters.

"Run," Agnes said, "and hurry."

They all three grabbed the hoops and sticks and ran. "Good-bye, Eloise. Come back earlier tomorrow," Marian called over her shoulder. "We can play some more."

"Yes," Eloise shouted, "I will."

Nancy Jane just kept running.

Eloise watched them go. They reached the edge of Tomstown and their awaiting duties. Eloise sank to the grass and sighed. Suddenly she was very lonely. It would be a long time until tomorrow. She had already grown especially fond of Marian, the older girl. A tiny unfamiliar ache arose within her where moments before laughter and happiness had bubbled.

In the distance to her left, two men labored. One was plowing Grandpa's field using a horse and some kind of plow with just one digger. The other man was using a mule to dislodge a large stump from the earth. A horse and mule, an old-looking town of stone and wood; no telephone poles, no road signs, no nothing; it was all very perplexing. They really needed electricity and telephones here.

Grandpa's pounding hammer in the barn caught her attention. How did he pass by her without her seeing him? Well, if she couldn't see her friends—especially her now best friend, Marian, she'd suddenly decided—until tomorrow, she'd ask Grandpa if she could watch him work from the doorway of the barn. And there was still that wonderful smell hanging in the air of freshly baked bread. She'd eat jam and bread and watch Grandpa. She leapt to her feet and ran toward the barn.

Turning the corner, she stubbed her toe on a stone and went down hard. There was a loud buzzing, then a ringing as her forehead struck a rock. After that she didn't know anything until she awoke in her bed with Grandma and Grandpa wearing very worried looks and an equally concerned-looking doctor standing over her.

"Just a nasty bruise," the doctor was saying. "Keep her down for at least two days. And keep her still."

Still? "I can't, Grandma." Eloise didn't recognize her own voice. It sounded scratchy and weak. "I met some new kids out back in town. We played 'rolling the hoop.' We're gonna play again, tomorrow. I promised."

"She's been dreaming," Grandpa said. His face creased with unease.

"You go to sleep, child," Grandma said sternly. "You'll be up soon enough." Her lips smiled, but her eyes didn't.

"But my friends," Eloise protested. "I told them I'd be there." She felt a bit of her strength returning and tried to sit up. It exhausted her and she fell back.

"There's no one there, honey," Grandma said. "Just an old field and woods."

"No! There's a town, Tomstown it's called, and men working and Marian and her sister Agnes, and Nancy Jane. They had to go milk the cow."

She watched her grandparents glance toward the doctor. "If she continues talking like this an hour from now, I want you to bring her to the hospital."

Hospital? Eloise didn't want to go to any old hospital. She was here on vacation. She was gonna stay here on vacation. In a couple of days when she could go out and play again, she'd see the girls and explain what had happened. Grandma was being an old fuddy-duddy. "You're right, Grandma, I guess I was dreaming. Do you think I could have some of your bread?"

"What bread, dear?" Grandma asked. She wiped Eloise's brow with a cool damp cloth.

"I smelled it baking this morning."

"I didn't bake this morning, Eloise." Again, Eloise saw in Grandma's eyes that questioning fear as she looked first at Grandpa and then at the doctor, who seemed unsure if leaving Eloise here was the right thing to do.

"Oh, that's right," Eloise said, quickly correcting herself. "That was in my dream too. I guess I should stay in bed and rest. Just like the doctor said."

Two days later she and Grandma took a walk out back. Eloise insisted on a noon picnic in the field and would hear of nothing else. She had been good for two whole days. She could scarcely contain herself as they walked around the side of the barn. She would not say: "See, Grandma, I told you there was a town." That would be rude, but she would giggle just a little.

As they rounded the corner, Eloise halted. Frantically, she looked around. "Grandma, where's the town?"

"There is no town, Eloise. I told you that."

"But I saw one, and over there . . ." She pointed to where the men had been working. "I watched a man plowing and another man using a mule to take out a tree." She ran to where she and the girls had played, to the exact spot where she had met the most wonderful friend in the world. Frantically, she cried, "Right here is where we played 'roll the hoop.' My friends, Marian and Agnes and Nancy Jane. Right here, Grandma! Their hoop was made out of wood, and they used sticks to roll it around. Right here, Grandma. My friend, Marian . . . right *here*!" She cried hysterically as her grandmother dropped the picnic basket and ran to her, scooping her into her arms.

Eloise grabbed Grandma around the neck and sobbed, her body racked with grief and loss.

During the rest of her stay, she frequented the field, wandering the length and breadth of it, ever watchful for the girls and the strange town. She spent a lot of time on her hands and knees in the area where they had played together, looking for clues that something had happened that fateful day. She showed Grandpa the nail she had found.

"It's old, all right," he'd said. "Likely forged by some blacksmith around here a long time ago."

The year was 1946, and Eloise Scott-Greenfield Webster, was almost ten years old.

Chapter One
1977

Eloise Scott-Greenfield Hamilton (when she married she dropped her father's surname, which her children now carried), stepped over a wide puddle stretching halfway across the earthen driveway as she exited the '71 Chevy. From the back seat, she grabbed her pocketbook and slung it over her shoulder while a heavy rain soaked her back. So much for May flowers, she thought grumpily. April had done its job with the rain thing, but May was falling down on its part.

Gathering up a bag of groceries intended to supplement this evening's supper, she listened with irritation to the overly loud TV. A blasting drumbeat thumped through her chest; *American Bandstand*? Nah. That was in the '50s and '60s. Something else then, but she didn't know what. The band's singing sounded like several people undergoing group surgery without benefit of anesthesia.

Upon entering the warm, well-lighted kitchen, she yelled, "Turn that damned thing down! Better yet, turn it off."

She loathed television, fervently believing that it robbed people of their minds and wallets without their ever being aware of it. TV ads! Nameless people on a screen invading her home, brainwashing adults and children to spend, spend, spend. She slammed the bag down on the counter and dropped her pocketbook onto a chair.

"Damn!" she snarled, thinking that if she used that word one more time tonight she'd kick herself. It was bad enough that her thirteen-year-old son, Bobby, occasionally used the word *crap*. Her language was horrendous tonight. Her daughter, Caroline, far more beautiful than any sixteen-year-old ought to be, and teetering on the edge of adulthood, was to have had the potatoes boiling and the chicken baking in the oven by now. The task not done was going to delay supper by an hour. Bob, her loving but very impatient husband, would have a fit. He hated waiting for supper. He hated waiting for *anything*.

Bob was a real estate dealer and a good one and did a brisk business by *not* waiting. He jumped on deals that no one else had the forethought to do. He was uncanny in his outlook on the housing market, whether it was buying or selling. He knew when to dump and when to grab. She was proud of his abilities, and quite immodestly, so was he.

"Damn!" she repeated.

She couldn't seem to get a grip on her foul mood this evening. Maybe it was this goddamn incessant rain and the mud that the dogs kept tracking in because they were digging up the lawn near the front walk. Why didn't Bob do something about it—like get rid of the dogs? Why did this family have two nutty beagles, anyway, that did nothing but eat, sleep on all the furniture and poop all over the yard, and sometimes in the house if the kids forgot to let them out before everybody went to bed for the night? They were nothing more than two animated, furry tubes. She was headed for the living room when that silly thought struck her. She sighed and leaned heavily against the doorjamb. God, she even hated Ira and Ike tonight, poor dogs. Her discomfort wasn't their fault.

She rubbed a weary hand across her face. It had been an unusually tough day. The nursing profession wasn't always as rewarding and glamorous as was once brightly promised on Career Day in her senior year of high school.

She waited until her anger subsided. The mutts were curled up together in one corner of the couch, their tails wagging for a second or two before flopping to a stop. They hadn't even bothered coming out to greet her today, likely because it was pouring outside. Smart dogs. At least they saved her from screaming at them all the way from the car to the foot of the stairs in the living room to quit jumping on her. All the while she'd be yelling, "Get your goddamned muddy paws off my whites."

The kids hadn't even heard her come in, the TV was blaring so, and they hadn't bothered sitting on the couch, a lovely flowered affair with a marble-topped coffee table in front of it. There was also Bob's Lazyboy recliner, twice as inviting as the sofa, just right for tired bodies. The end tables beside the couch and chair held reading lamps, family photos and empty soda bottles, which made Eloise sigh tiredly. A few braided rag rugs were scattered on the hardwood floor. The walls, a plain wallpaper print, were set off with a few framed prints of homey scenes.

Eloise watched the TV for several seconds. On a couple of different occasions, she'd tried watching the show with them, suffering through an hour of live singers with deadpan expressions singing about love, sex and murder in an effort to "bond" more closely with viewers. Yeah, right! Truth to tell, it was to sell records and tapes. She'd despised the show. The kids knew she'd despised it, and when she rose from the couch saying, "Not bad, kids," they knew she was lying through her teeth.

The fact that it was Friday was the one redeeming feature of the evening. As much as she loved her patients and as often as she went out of her way for them—above and beyond the call of duty, she was often told by her supervisor—she wouldn't have to wipe one old person's bottom or empty one kidney basin or a single bedpan before eight AM Monday morning. The thought sent tiny shivers of excitement racing through her, raising her spirits at least as high as her kneecaps.

Bobby, who was already taking on weight around his midriff, glanced up from the floor where he lay sprawled in front of the tube, his head resting at an unhealthy angle against the couch.

"You're going to be sterile before you're fifteen," she told him frankly. Color television was reputed to do that to males. It was not yet proven, but she did want to be a grandmother someday.

He winced. "Aw, Mom, that's a lot of crap. Dad told me so."

She stiffened, but she let his slang slide. She had faced enough confrontation for one day.

Yes, and wasn't it true that whatever Daddy said was Gospel, whereas whatever she told them was often subject to question? She hadn't doubted one thing her parents had told her before she was fifteen or sixteen, or, for that matter, her grandparents, except for that one single time out back of their barn when she thought she'd seen . . . well, whatever it was she'd seen. It didn't matter anyway. The barn, destroyed by a lightning fire years ago, was long gone and so, pretty much, was the memory—except for the warmth it still brought to her whenever she recalled the "phantom incident," as she had come to think of it.

"Take my word for it, Bobby." Get the last word in. That was the important thing.

Leaning against the far end of the couch, Caroline also sat on the floor, the phone plastered against her ear.

"Caroline," Eloise called over the bombastic TV while gallantly trying to project patience, witticism and humor into her voice. "Could you please unglue yourself from the phone for a moment? Bobby, turn down the TV, please. I can't hear myself think."

He gave her a sullen look but did as he was asked, reaching with a medium-sized ham-like hand and turning down the volume.

So like his father, Eloise thought. Scary. Already big and brawny like Bob, he'd be playing football in another year and likely knocking over anyone and everyone directly in his path. He was going to be a star. Stylishly, and in spite of his increasing weight, a gray sweatshirt and blue jeans hung like loose grain sacks on his frame. Already he was shaving his upper lip. Most of his classmates probably didn't yet own a razor. He wore his dark brown hair in a shag. If he stood, he'd be two inches taller than her, and she was five feet seven.

She and her daughter were much alike in their physical makeup. Tall and thin, they both had large, blue eyes and golden-brown hair. Their teeth were perfect, thanks to thousands of dollars of dental work on them both. For convenience and speed Eloise wore her hair bobbed while Caroline's flowed in natural waves down to the small of her back. Caroline's cheekbones bore a few superficial scars from a light case of acne, which she fretted over a great deal, but those were the only flaws in her otherwise perfect appearance. Eloise was proud that her figure still matched that of her daughter's, but she knew she'd never have Caroline's tight, flat belly again.

Caroline muttered something into the phone, then dropped it onto the cradle. Pivoting around on well shaped buttocks, she rested her elbows on her knees; she was wearing what Eloise considered dangerously blood-constricting blue jeans and a skin-tight, mint-green sleeveless top showing off size-B breasts, of which she was inordinately proud. "Yes?" Her eyes challenged her mother.

"The potatoes, dear. Weren't you going to have them started by now? And have the chicken in the oven? You know how your father hates a late supper."

"He's not coming home."

Eloise's tiny bit of positive excitement slipped a notch. She had been looking forward to seeing him. "Oh? Did he call?"

Caroline's eyebrows slowly arched. Such drama, Eloise thought, embarrassed for her.

"He won't be home till late. I don't know why. Just said he'd be real late."

19

Obviously, an unexpected real estate opportunity had opened up.

Well, a brief statement, if no further intelligent conversation from Caroline, was better than nothing from her. Her daughter had been brisk toward her mother since she was ten years old—when her period began or, more aptly put these days, when she began to "bleed." Eloise hated that delineation. It sounded as though Caroline were dying from loss of blood. Maybe, Eloise thought, I've been a nurse for too long.

Eloise nodded that she understood Bob's message and pursed her lips. "All right, then, honey," she said brightly, thinking she sounded ridiculously like Mary Poppins. "Let's get the chicken going, shall we? I'll go change my clothes and be right down to help."

"Can't," Caroline said. "I'm staying overnight at Betsy's house. Can I take the car? I'm supposed to be there now." She'd taken driver's ed. She could legally drive at night.

"Yeah, Mom," Bobby said in a voice that was more like yelling than speaking normally as he exercised his maturing manhood with his ever-deepening baritone. "I'm going over to Fritz's tonight. We're gonna watch basketball."

"How are you planning to get there, Bobby?" Eloise asked him.

Bobby looked a little surprised. "Caroline, here," he said, directing a thumb toward his sister. "She's gonna drop me off. Fritz's dad'll bring me back afterward."

Caroline nodded, agreeing.

Obviously the evening had already been planned. Eloise, however, was the one who held the keys to the car, which she alone had bought and paid for. She breathed deeply, stalling. She could say no and live with their anger and sullenness throughout the rest of the evening and well into tomorrow while trying to mollify them, or she could give in, knowing she couldn't win. On the other hand, she could gain a peaceful, albeit lonely, evening. Her chest constricted with an aching sadness. She didn't want to spend another Friday evening alone! This would be the third or maybe it was the fourth time in a row that this had happened.

Her children looked expectantly at her, waiting, knowing the answer before she did. "The keys are in my coat pocket. Be careful driving, Caroline. Be home by noon." The house emptied within two minutes. Eloise turned off the TV and listened to the car leaving the driveway.

She flopped down on the couch next to the beagles and absently began to stroke the bundles of black and tan fur. She didn't blame the kids for wanting to go out. They lived so far from their friends, seeing them mainly at school.

Much to everyone's surprise, but to no one's disapproval since her grandparents' children were still content living in large cities in distant places, Eloise had, with her parents' help and blessings, purchased the farm after Grandma and Grandpa's deaths. At twenty years old, she became the sole owner of the fifty-five-acre farm on Dutch Hill Road, with prime land, good pasturing and a nice little creek running on the far side of the meadow. Located just outside the tiny village of Frankfort Center, the farm was quiet with the nearest human contact three-quarters of a mile away. It was a little less than an hour's drive in either direction to Utica or Frankfort where she worked as a nurse on a geriatric ward. Ilion and Herkimer were not much farther beyond Frankfort.

Her parents had helped her lease and care for the farmhouse until she had graduated from nursing school at the University of Buffalo. Following graduation, she promptly returned, living alone until she married at age twenty-four, insisting that she and Bob make the farm their permanent residence. She added his name to the deed, and they settled in to raise a family.

Bob's reluctant willingness to live in this relatively secluded spot was one of the few concessions she could ever recall his making. He was a Utica city-boy all the way and so strong-minded that, to this day, she thanked her lucky stars that she'd stuck to her guns on this one. Lord knows, she'd won few battles with him since then.

She wandered back to the kitchen and put away the groceries. For supper she ate Cheerios drenched in milk and loaded down with the last of the frozen blueberries left over from last summer's picking. She was hungry enough, but she was in no mood to cook.

After tidying the kitchen, she drifted to the living room and curled up with the beagles. They were good company even if she didn't like them all the time. She stared through the glass double doors leading out onto a small cedar deck. She hadn't wanted the living room wall invaded with a French door or a deck of any kind. She wanted to preserve the place just as her grandparents had left it. Since moving in twenty years ago, she had had the entire dwelling newly painted and rewired, the plumbing upgraded, an upstairs bath added for everyone's use, a new septic system installed, the walls reinsulated and new windows put in, but everything else concerning the house's structure was still much the same as it had been since the mid-1800s—with the exception of Bob's insistence upon the modern doors and deck. She couldn't convince her mind's eye that the change to the house was attractive, but everyone else loved it.

Bob often liked to barbeque out there, and the kids enjoyed having their friends over and hanging out on the deck while playing their boom boxes cranked high. Those were the nights she left Bob in charge and escaped into Ilion to the library or to lectures held at the Ilion and Herkimer museums on whatever subject might strike her interest.

Though it was still daylight, every lamp in the room was burning. She rose and turned off all but one small table lamp beside the couch. With dusk approaching, its light emitted a warm glow through its pink glass shade.

Resting her elbows on her knees and propping her head on her fists, she stared through the door until the day completely faded. The rain had ceased during the past hour but was beginning again. Normally soothing, the downpour grated against her nerves. She wished it were high noon—summertime—with the sun blazing down upon her. She wished she were nine years old again so that she could run wild out back of the barn where there was still a large, grassy meadow and woods to explore for hours on end.

Once, but only once, there had been three little girls who had played in the field with her from the town called . . . She strived to remember its name. Tomstown. Yes, that was it. A funny name to call a town, she thought. She recalled each child as though having seeing her only moments before. It was remarkable how she remembered their names and how she particularly missed Marian even after all this time. The old village, too, was still vivid in her mind. And now there was that awful deck and offensive French doors not unlike a large glass wound in the house's east wall, detracting from earlier, happier times.

She supposed there were compensations in being alone tonight. She need not worry about her temperamental kids or fixing Bob's supper. Tired of brooding and bored with looking at the rectangular black panes reflecting back her image, she rose and wandered around the house, touching this and that knickknack while contemplating how, at forty years of age, she had reached this insufferably dull stage of life. She had wanted to do so much more, to see so many things, to experience *life* before she'd settled down. Maybe she had already experienced her great encounter and somehow missed it. Yet, how could she complain? She had two beautiful, healthy, intelligent, darned near grown-up children and a loving husband. A bit domineering and critical, he was nonetheless faithful, and that was more than most of her friends could say about their husbands.

She was always somewhat in awe of Bob's interaction with the kids. Occasionally when he addressed them, it sounded as though he were speaking to a couple of windup dolls, actual possessions programmed to perform certain acts upon command. "Clean your room," he would say, and both kids would jump to do his bidding. "Get to bed by ten," and off they'd march right on time, every time. It wasn't that he was gruff toward them. It was just his way of speaking, his voice, his delivery. It certainly unnerved her. Maybe it did the kids, too, but if not, then it had to be respect for their father, something she believed they did not have for her. More than once she'd tried using Bob's approach; a hundred times, a thousand times, and it never worked. The kids snapped back at her. Speaking sharply or pleasantly to them wasn't any better. They still snapped. She didn't know what they wanted, how to reach them. She didn't even know how to reach Bob except by making sure the house was always clean and that meals were served on time. That made him smile, made him reach for her. She felt loved then.

An impatient snort escaped her. She was a *modern* woman! She had her nails done once every two weeks; she had her own shrink, as did all her friends, that she saw every couple of weeks, and her own trainer at the health club where, when occasionally she had the extra energy, she worked out. This was the year 1977, for God's sake. How had she reached such a level of discontentment? Lord, if she went any further with this line of thinking she'd be so depressed she wouldn't be able to drag her bones upstairs to bed.

For sure, there'd been some big, big changes in this old house since she had been nine years old.

Chapter Two

Eloise slept away for the better part of the weekend. Whenever she did get up, for a cup of tea or something to eat, she slipped her feet into a pair of battered sheep's wool-lined slippers that she couldn't part with and pulled on a fuzzy, white terry cloth bathrobe. The robe was old and worn, but it was her comfort blanket with big deep pockets into which she could bury her hands when they were cold.

Apparently sensing her need for rest, her family had had the good sense to leave her to herself throughout the weekend. Now it was Monday morning, and the entire family's "nothing out of the ordinary" breakfast ritual was noisily taking place. Simultaneously, they were making so many demands on her that her head began to throb. She pulled her robe tighter to her body, drawing solace from its soft bulkiness.

"I'd like dinner on the table as soon as I get home, honey." Bob's voice boomed off the walls. "I've got an anxious client I have to meet in Frankfort this evening by eight sharp." Even in his home life, timing was everything to him. He snapped the Utica *Observer Dispatch* upright before him. The sound exploded in her ears. She suspected she was running a slight fever.

"Of course, dear," Eloise said, pouring him coffee. She returned the pot to the stove.

"Can I have ten dollars, Mom?" Caroline asked in a low voice, thank God, but her lower lip protruded slightly, her tan brows deeply furrowed as she openly sulked even while asking for money. Of course, she was angry because she couldn't have the car tonight to go over to Jen's and study for a coming exam. "I need it for a down payment on my class ring."

"You're only a junior, Caroline," Eloise reminded her.

"Yeah, but they wanna make sure that next year's seniors are really gonna buy their rings. This sorta guarantees them that."

"Guarantees whom?" Eloise sat down to eat her toast.

Caroline sighed in exasperation. She placed an impatient hand on her slender hip and looked at her mother as though she knew nothing. "You know. The company that makes the rings."

"Yeah, Ma," Bobby said loudly, speaking as though he were several rooms removed from her. He tore around the kitchen, opening and slamming cupboard doors. "I gotta have five bucks for lunch. Where the heck's the corn flakes? I gotta have something to eat before the bus gets here, for crying out loud." The beagles leaped around his legs, begging him to feed them.

Eloise closed her eyes as her mind screamed, Why don't you kids ask your father? And you, Caroline, she wanted to say, should at least have the decency to suck up to your mother a little while you're begging her for money *and* her car. In a contest of wills, Eloise endured Caroline's sullenness. She had no excuse for refusing her daughter the car other than she liked to believe that she still had some control over her own automobile.

She reached for her coffee. Damn! She should have refilled her cup when she was pouring Bob's. As she rounded the table to get the pot, she tripped over the beagles, who were jumping and walking around on their hind legs to make themselves taller (and just who the hell taught them that obnoxious trick?) and still demanding to be fed. As she poured the coffee, she stepped backward, bumping against a chair to avoid their dirty paws landing on her. Hot coffee sloshed across her hand.

"Bobby," she shouted, "feed these damned mutts. Do it out on the porch." She breathed deeply checking her rising temper.

Bobby continued ransacking the cupboards. "Where's the Wheaties?"

"*Bobby!*"

"I gotta eat, Mom! The bus'll be here any minute."

Setting down the pot, she snapped at him. "You should have thought of that when I called you an hour ago, instead of lying in bed for another forty-five minutes." At the sink she doused her hand beneath cold water and appealed to Bob, who was sipping coffee, completely absorbed in the morning paper. "Bob, *please*, tell him to do as he's told." She felt her increasing anger reddening her cheeks.

Without raising his voice or his eyes, he said, "Bobby."

Bobby jumped to the task.

How did Bob do that? Eloise looked to see if there was fear in her son's eyes. There wasn't. He wasn't a bit afraid of his father.

"Caroline," Bob continued softly, while still concentrating on the paper, "help your mother."

"How?" Caroline whined, displaying a bit more grit than her brother. She looked helplessly around the untidy kitchen.

Eloise was vastly relieved to hear Bob speak to Caroline as well. Last night's orderly table was now cluttered with schoolbooks, breakfast dishes, sections of this morning's paper. The countertops were cluttered with Caroline's half-prepared lunch, spilled coffee grounds, a couple of boxes of cereal that Bobby had completely over-looked. Given five minutes and half a chance, this family could be capable of destroying the entire infrastructure of any given country at a moment's notice.

She dried her hand on a towel hanging over a chair and sat again at the table, the same one her grandmother had used for years. A four-burner gas stove had replaced the old General Electric. Tall cupboards extending from mid-wall to ceiling with large and deep sturdily built-in drawers beneath were still in place. Throughout the house all exposed trim was hickory—cupboards, casings, doors and bannister, the darkened wood adding warmth and depth to the house. Floors and stairs were wide, oaken planks sanded and finished to a fine gleam. Long ago, Grandpa had painted the trim in the kitchen a glossy white, but soon after moving in, Eloise had stripped the wood, reexposing its rich color. The kitchen linoleum had also been replaced with tile. By the time Eloise took up residence, too many years' footsteps had devastated Grandma's "plastic rug," as she always called it. First the fake, brown blocks had rubbed away, then holes began appearing before the sink and stove and around the table. The ugly, black, linseed oil-soaked burlap below had surfaced. Eventually, even that wore through, revealing the broad, unfinished planks beneath. Overhead, Grandpa's beautiful handiwork still remained: a tin ceiling of pressed flower-pattern blocks painted white, installed when Grandma first married and moved in with her husband and his family sixty-seven years ago. The walls were repainted a pale green. Eloise had balked at installing a dishwasher. It just did not fit this room. She considered the kitchen her soul room. Normally, it was the one room in the entire house that brought her more comfort than any other. Today that wasn't happening.

"Dishes, Caroline," Bob said, finally looking up. "Clean up around here. Help your mother and get them started."

Oh, good grief, Eloise thought. "It's too late for Caroline to help out now," she said, feeling that she must intervene. "Just put them in the sink, Caroline. There really isn't enough time to wash—"

"Start the water," Bob said quietly. His tone demanded obedience. Feeling like she herself was being scolded, Eloise bit her lower lip and kept still as Caroline turned on the tap and slid some bowls and spoons into the rising suds.

Eloise nibbled on her toast. Now that her daughter was making herself useful, she wasn't any happier, but in a few minutes they'd all be gone, including the dogs, now already out of the house thanks to Bobby's fast work. That would leave her ten wonderfully, peaceful minutes alone before dressing. She would sit and watch the sun continue to rise. Correction: She'd watch the low-flying, thick gray clouds pass overhead.

She consciously refrained from shaking her head as a sense of despondency settled over her. Working on the geriatric ward, she frequently found it an exceedingly depressing place to be. For nineteen years she had been there. Initially, she had loved her job, enjoying making old people feel better both physically and mentally and better about sometimes being alone without family or friends. She made promises to them to visit everyday that they were there, and she willingly did it even if it meant working without pay beyond her normal hours.

For several years she was head nurse, but the job demanded more time from her than regular nursing had, and so she gave up the better paying position. She excelled at her tasks and was cheerful all the time, with assurances to everybody that they were going to be fine, that they'd soon be back home, even when she knew she was lying. Well, she didn't feel cheerful anymore. Too many years, too many deaths.

The bus tooted. Eloise looked at her watch. Seven on the dot, and thank God.

Hastily, the kids pecked their mother on the cheek, yelling as they did so, "'Bye, Mom, 'bye Dad." Caroline took time to quickly kiss her dad, but Bobby had long ago stopped such intimate affection to one of his own sex.

Eloise's ears rang as the kids bolted through the screen door, its hinges as squeaky as ever, and off the back porch. They sailed off the steps like she had done when she was a child.

She spoke to the newspaper wall separating her from her husband. "Those kids should have been out there by now. Not waiting until the bus had to honk its horn three times to get them moving." She took a sip of coffee, her mind obsessing on their lazy behavior. "They don't act like they're even nearing adulthood."

"Sure they do," came an answer from behind the paper barrier. "You've watched the old *Father Knows Best* and *Ozzie and Harriet* reruns."

"Not in years. And nobody acts like that anymore," she answered impatiently. "And they probably didn't then, either."

"Well, be glad these two do. Most kids don't even see their parents in the morning." The paper rustled, and the room grew quiet again.

How would he know, barricaded behind his newspaper every morning? At least when the kids were little, Bob had spent a couple of hours each evening in front of the tube with them. Bobby would snuggle against one side of his dad, and Caroline against the other, and Bob's strong arms would cuddle them both tightly against him. But now Bobby and Caroline were old children, and Bob's attention toward them had waned. She was certain that he already saw them as adults. If only they weren't such physically mature children. She sighed. Sometimes she herself had trouble remembering.

Bob folded the paper and set it aside. He swallowed the last of his coffee and pushed back his chair. Preparing to go, he gave his sharply creased pants a hitch, then slid into a matching navy suit coat over a white sports shirt. He was a handsome man. Slightly balding at the crown, his black hair still had women envying its natural waves. His eyes, set off by thick black eyebrows, were gray and flashing; his teeth, false from a years-ago, head-on car collision one drunken night, were, of course, perfect. He had thickened a bit with the arrival of his mid-forties, but his body still rippled, and his abs were still fairly well intact. Eloise smiled at him, loving him fiercely at that moment.

"Later," he murmured against her hair, nuzzling her in a surprising show of affection. He picked up his keys and headed for the front door. "Don't forget," he reminded her. "Early supper. On time."

"Fine, dear," she said, following him. "It'll be ready."

She returned to the empty kitchen to finish her coffee. The love she felt for Bob moments ago began fading. She struggled to maintain her ardor, but it drained from her as easily as the rain now poured from the clouds. Unexpected tears blurred her vision. What was *wrong* with her?

"Oh, screw it!" she muttered. Without guilt, she went to the phone and called in sick. That done, she looked at the soaking dishes. "And screw you too." For once she'd first go do something she wanted to do around here.

Upstairs in the master bedroom, she made up the queen-sized bed, straightening the sheets and quilt, then retrieved her jewelry box from the large oak bureau graced with an equally wide and tall mirror. She sat on the edge of the bed for a moment looking around the room. The furniture was heavy and expensive. Filled with extra linens, a cedar chest sat at the end of the bed. A window opposite the bed lighted the room. There was a closet on the left, with the entryway to the right. Matching oak nightstands held small Tiffany lamps and remote controls for the electric blanket. The floor was carpeted wall to wall with a thick tan rug. It was a comfortable room, its color scheme and heavy furniture reminding Eloise of a bear's den. She thought the room too masculine, but she liked its aura of strength and protectiveness.

She turned her attention to the teak box on her lap. Opening it, she viewed an array of jewelry amassed within the box's blue velvet interior. She began to sort out a rat's nest of gold and silver chains, earrings and a dozen or so pins and broaches intertwined amongst the chains.

At the bottom of the case, she came across the square-sided iron nail she'd found the summer she'd met, or at least thought she had

31

met, three little girls in Grandma and Grandpa's hayfield. There wasn't much left of the old peg anymore, little pieces of it having broken off over the years from being carelessly tossed about in the jewelry box. Studying the tiny spike, she pursed her lips. Today was "clean out the jewelry box day," and the nail, nothing more than junk actually, was added to several pieces of cheap paste she no longer wanted and knew Caroline wouldn't care for, either.

Pocketing the discards in her bathrobe, she felt good about having tidied up the mess. Returning the box to the dresser, she decided to hit the closet next. In it were several pairs of white Red Cross shoes that were no longer fit to wear at the hospital. Not one for wearing soft-soled shoes anywhere else, Eloise had let them stack up in one corner of the closet. With the old footwear destined for the garbage bin, she thought she was ready to face the dishes now. Her heavy mood had lifted, leaving her to believe that she could probably endure the rest of the day without too much fuss.

She dug the junked baubles from her pocket and dumped them and the sneakers into the trash can outside the back door, then returned to test the dishwater. It had chilled, so she drew fresh hot water, then idly washed the dishes and gazed through the window over the kitchen sink.

With the barn now gone, her view of the wonderful meadow was unobstructed. A neighboring farmer used it as a crop field, this year planting alfalfa. The woods beyond the meadow were still big, deep and timeless. She was so very thankful that she lived here, that her grandparents had realized how much she loved the place. Now and then, the very fact of it exhilarated her.

Thankfully, the rain had stopped, the massive, ominous clouds finally breaking up. A welcoming ray of sunshine stole through a slate-gray hole in the sky and turned the meadow from a drab olive to a rich, park-bench green. Eloise smiled, already feeling a change in the atmosphere. Fifteen minutes later, the sky was nearly clear, and a warm sun beat down upon the house.

Still dallying at the sink she suddenly began to sweat. She cranked open the dual-casement window to let in fresh air—and heat. It could never get too hot for her. She stretched, reaching across the sink to playfully stick her hand out the window, just so she could feel *no* rain falling. The most pleasant aroma of baking bread wafted in.

She laughed at herself and looked out across the sparkling field. A sharp breath escaped her as she stared in utter astonishment. She blinked several times, her hand still extended, forgotten as though it were no longer a part of her body. On the far side of the field was the same town she had once seen as a child. The clustered houses, cows grazing in the pasture, plus a few more buildings infringed upon the field. The town had seemed so much farther away, back then. But she had been just a little girl, and things always looked so much different when one saw them years later.

She looked for children playing in the grass, but there were none. A man was plowing with a single-bladed plow, a horse pulling the implement. Quite far down the main street behind a stone house, it looked like a woman was working in a backyard garden. A great exultation filled her chest to bursting as she absently withdrew her hand. As she did the scene began to fade.

"No!" she cried. "Don't go."

She grabbed the window ledge, clutching the sill as though her fierce grip could stop the scene from disappearing. The vision reappeared as strong as ever. Her face twisted in consternation as she eyed her hand as though it were a thing unto itself, an object that created life on its own. At this moment she feared her hand, her stomach filling with bile, her head beginning to whirl. She battled a great temptation to bolt from there; to run upstairs and hide like a frightened child beneath the bed. The moment passed, and with trepidation, she slowly lifted her hand from the sill. Again the town began to fade. Sweat poured off her face, rolled down her back, soaking her shirt. She was going crazy. She knew it. She felt as though she were peeing in her pants and quickly looked down at herself. She was dry, which left her little consoled.

Renewed terror raged through her as she again grasped the sill. The town came back into full focus. She refused to give in to her fear, gripping the wood harder yet. It seemed that as long as she touched the sill the town would remain. This time she didn't let go, and the village stayed put.

She watched wide-eyed as two women, dressed in eighteenth century garb, left one of the stone row houses located toward the nearer end of town. The ladies wore loose-fitting tan and white dresses from neck to ground. Small white hats were perched upon their heads. Their hair appeared short; most likely it was braided in coils and pinned up under their hats. They exited through a picket gate, turned left and walked up the dirt street in the direction of Eloise's field.

Her hand still locked in place, from fear or fascination, Eloise wasn't sure which, she noted more details while continuing to awkwardly cling to the sill. Actually, she didn't dare move. She was that sure she was going to faint.

Astoundingly, through the field appeared a well-worn footpath she had never before seen, leading toward her house. Walking briskly along the path, each woman held a cloth-covered basket draped over her arm. Eloise could hear them laughing and chatting as they drew nearer. Unable to distinguish what they were saying, the mere fact that she could now *hear* as well as see them sent renewed bolts of panic galloping through her veins. She was completely convinced that she was going crazy right here and now.

The women came closer. Now she could discern their brown eyes and graying brown hair. Their dresses were made of a faded brown, coarse linen.

They approached the house, then turned left, disappearing around the west side of the building and out of sight. Eloise released the sill and hoisted herself onto the sink, straining to see out of the window, searching for them. Quite suddenly, the town began to fade. She dropped to the floor and again grabbed the sill, returning the town's image. Awkward though her arm felt as she continued to stretch toward the window, she kept her hand soundly anchored as though it were part of the sill itself. The town remained as she turned her attention toward the screen door.

Impossible! There stood the women before it.

Through the screen came the taller one's voice, clearly and musically, asking, "Have you baked morning bread yet?"

As the question was asked, Eloise involuntarily released the sill and collapsed like a rag doll onto the floor, the pungent smell of baking bread strong in the air.

Chapter Three

Eloise came to in a heap on the floor. A strong breeze brushed against her face as a gust of wind blew open the screen door; it tapped, tapped, tapped against the outside wall. Then it all came rushing back to her: the vision of a bygone town, men laboring in the field, two women coming to her door.

One actually speaking to her . . .

Slowly, she half-rose, glancing toward the door. It continued banging against the siding, but no one stood at the threshold. Though overwhelmingly dizzy and slightly nauseous, she felt she must look outside to see what was there. She crawled to the sink, hauled herself up and peered over the window's edge. There was nothing out there but an empty field. No town, no people. Nothing!

Rapidly, she cranked closed the window and locked it. She would lock the screen door too, lock *all* the doors and go back to bed and sleep. She was tired and overwrought, that was all. The kids were getting to her. Bob was getting to her. Even the dogs that she normally loved were driving her crazy.

She secured the house, both downstairs and up. If she were to rest, she must feel safe. She went to bed and was asleep within minutes.

Waking at noon, she felt one hundred percent better. She rose, showered, revised her decision to take the day off, donned her uniform and headed for the hospital. It would be better than staying at home and thinking. She drove with the windows opened wide and the radio playing Led Zeppelin at top volume.

Over the next few days, Eloise settled into what she considered the old comfortable routine—the kids yammering at her; Bob his demanding and exacting self; and the beagles continuously underfoot. In fact, she welcomed the chaos, happily embracing her family life, thriving on her hectic eight-to-four schedule, working a tough job, seeing her counselor every couple of weeks as usual just to give her somebody to talk to, to *really* talk to, and working out more frequently at the health club. She was able to pet the dogs again and sleep cuddled next to Bob each night. One evening she even managed to talk the kids into taking in a movie with her, given that she let them choose the one they wanted to see. She hated the film—all those killings and multiple car crashes—but the kids loved it. It was the time spent with them that she cherished. And she stayed away from the kitchen sink window. Regrettably, her euphoria didn't last.

As soon as her eyes opened this Wednesday morning, she experienced a sense of foreboding. Something was going to happen today. She could feel it in her bones as her heart began to race.

The morning went along smoothly enough. At the breakfast table, she heard from the other side of the *Observer Dispatch*, "Honey, supper on time tonight. And Jim Alden's joining us. I need to convince him that buying a house in Ilion is a smart move."

From Bobby: "I can't find the cereal."

As sweet as could be, Caroline lovingly draped herself over her father's shoulder, saying, "Can I have five dollars for lunch today, Dad?"

Eloise barely suppressed a snigger. For once, Caroline had asked her father. She tried to feel badly for any past rotten attitudes she'd harbored toward Caroline, but she couldn't. Kids could be nasty little things, even with their parents never wanting to believe it possible.

She stopped thinking like that. Morbid feelings crashed in on her as she moaned and rested her head against her hand. The smell of the cereal before her nauseated her.

Alerted, Caroline glanced at her mother. "You sick, Mom?"

Bob lowered the paper. "What's up?"

"She's pregnant," Bobby announced. He could hardly stand up straight, he was laughing so hard.

"Shut up," Bob yelled at him. Bobby sobered instantly. He found the cereal he'd been searching for and grabbed a bowl from the dish drainer. Bob turned back to Eloise. "Are you all right, honey?"

If there was one thing she could say about Bob, it was his quick attention to her if she didn't feel well. She raised her head. "I'm fine, dear. Just a little bug."

Bobby smirked and Caroline attacked him. "You stupid jerk. Shut the hell up!"

"Caroline!" Eloise exploded. "Watch your language."

Bob looked sharply at his daughter. She withered beneath his glare.

"I'm fine," Eloise assured them all with a weak smile. "Just settle down, everybody. This isn't helping anything."

Bob scowled, apparently thinking he was included in Eloise's scolding, but he said, "Your mother's right. Just get your breakfast, and go on out and wait for the bus. You don't have to be late every day. In fact," he said pointedly, folding his paper, a sure warning sign to them all, "from now on when your mother calls you in the morning, one, get up and get ready for school; two, eat your breakfast; and three, go outside and be there *before* the bus comes. That understood?" He looked at each of his children, holding eye contact with them until he got the requisite nods.

"But what if I need to talk to you or Mom about something?" Caroline whined. "What am I supposed to do? Leave a note?"

Eloise could see Bob simmering just beneath the surface. He answered quietly. "If we are unavailable the previous evening to talk to you, then yes, a note will do fine. But I doubt that'll happen since it never has so far. Otherwise, talk to us while you are sitting at the table, eating your breakfast. Do you have any questions, Bobby?"

"No, Dad." Bobby kept his life simple at tense moments like these. Eloise admired his wisdom but wondered from time to time if he were being beaten into submission without his realizing it.

Bob rattled the paper, recreating his wall. The children slunk around, eating quickly and getting out as soon as possible. Without Bob's noticing, Eloise slipped her daughter two fives. Caroline nodded, understanding that she was to say nothing and that one of the bills was to go to her brother.

The screen door slammed behind them.

Bob lay aside the paper then rinsed his cup at the sink. Gazing through the window, he said, "It's going to be a hot one today." He threw his suit coat over his arm and grabbed his keys from the table. "I'll see you later," he said, giving Eloise a kiss and a hug. "Feel better." She drank in his affection as though she were dying of thirst and watched him disappear out the door.

She glanced at the clock; she should leave, but she could squeeze in one more quick cup of coffee if she cooled it down with a little cold water. She poured at the stove, cooled at the sink, then returned to the table, taking much more time than she ought, letting her thoughts play around in her head while she sipped. She felt better since Bob showed that little bit of tenderness. He was usually so anxious to leave that he always surprised her whenever he added a nice little hug to his morning ritual.

She reached for a pencil among the usual clutter scattered across the morning table. She drew the newspaper toward her and, her mind still wandering, began to doodle in the margins. A human stick figure appeared, then an animal that could have been anything from a dog to a cow; next, a smiley face. The smiley face drew her interest, and she added a few details. She erased the typical grin and drew eyes, nose and lips. Something hung on the edge of her consciousness. She frowned thoughtfully and changed the shape of the head, making it more oval, adding a cap and curls jutting out around the hat. She studied the tiny portrait. It needed something to complete it, some little thing. Without knowing why, she carefully drew a single line no more than a millimeter long down the center of the chin.

"Cleft chin, cleft chin. Why does that remind me of something?" she mused aloud.

In a rush, she remembered: the town—and the ladies approaching her house.

Gasping, she thrust herself away from the table. The pencil flew as coffee spilled across the top. Chills rolled like wintery gusts over her body.

Somehow the newspaper was spared the coffee mishap, and she stared, trembling, at her crude drawing. The miniature face looked up at her. It wasn't a good likeness, not by a long shot, but it was accurate enough so that Eloise recognized the taller of the two women she'd seen at her kitchen door only a few days ago.

"*Stupid!*" she shouted at the image. "This whole thing is just plain stupid. I never saw a thing." She whirled away from the table and stamped her way through the living room and up the stairs, stopping long enough to viciously brush her teeth, ditch her slippers and pull on her Red Cross whites. She drove like a lunatic all the way to work.

By the time she returned home that evening, she fully accepted that she had, in fact, experienced the two strange happenings; the one when she'd been a child, and the more recent one, the one that occurred last week. At least a child, she thought ruefully, could plausibly have experienced make-believe friends.

She spoke to her psychologist about it for the first time that Wednesday. "It's so real, Dr. Strictland. Like I'm really there." She corrected herself. "I *am* there! And those people are there too."

Dr. Strictland said nothing, watching her with affable eyes.

"Aren't you going to say anything?" Eloise asked impatiently. "I just told you that I saw into the past. Am I going crazy, or what?"

Tiny, dark-haired and extremely well-dressed Dr. Rosa D. Strictland, Ph.D., shifted slightly in her black, leather-upholstered chair. Silver earrings dangled from her lobes. Her dark eyes shown, and her smile could melt hearts. The skirt of her blue silk dress rustled slightly. Black sandals adorned her naked feet.

The walls of her office were graced with expensively framed degrees from Cornell University, UCLA and NYU as well as the University of St. Andrews in Scotland. Only an aging and ailing mother kept her in Ilion. Otherwise, she'd once mentioned to Eloise, she'd be in New York City, right now.

The office was opulent. None of its furnishings—desk, brown leather couch and three large tan leather chairs—came cheaply. One small window set rather high in the wall allowed in the only light. Soft wattage in glass lamps on small cherry, marble-topped tables illuminated the room. The entire effect was for the sake of the client, to create a sense of calm in the confining environment. It wasn't working for Eloise.

"You've talked about this for the entire session, Eloise," Dr. Strictland said in her ever-noncommittal voice. "You believe it. You even say you were directly involved part of the time."

"*Every* time," Eloise insisted.

"Every time," Strictland agreed. "You're a bright woman not given to fantasies. At least not during the two years you've been working with me. My suggestion to you would be that we continue talking about this. Meanwhile, since you firmly believe in what you saw, I could send you to an independent psychologist who could test you . . ."

41

Eloise's eyes flared. "I beg your pardon?"

"Only to determine if there is some kind of a breakdown occurring, Eloise, although I don't believe it for one minute. We could also set up a C/T scan—"

"A *CAT* scan? You want to scan my brain?"

Dr. Strictland went on as if she had not been interrupted. "To look for a possible physiological cause. I'd also suggest having a full physical workup done as well."

Irritably, Eloise snapped, "I had a physical two months ago. I'm as fit as a fiddle."

"All right, then," Strictland calmly replied. "You're fine. You don't hear things. You don't see things. You never played with three little girls from long ago." She rested the clipboard in her lap, paused, then repeated, "You're fine."

Eloise dissolved into tears and buried her face in her hands. "What if I am going crazy, Dr. Strictland? What if I'm a schizophrenic, and it's only now beginning to manifest itself?"

"You weren't a schizophrenic when you were nine years old, were you?" Strictland asked quietly. "Its onset isn't unusual in one so young or even much younger, but, if I may say so without seeming insulting, it seldom occurs in one so old as yourself."

Eloise's hands dropped. "Well, at least reaching my forties accounts for something positive," she said, dabbing at her eyes, trying to be humorous and knowing she wasn't. "All right, then, rule that one out, but for God's sake, come up with something. You're the doctor."

The room was quiet for a moment before Dr. Strictland responded. "Let's get those tests done and go from there. We'll let the physical go, at least for the time being."

Eloise nodded, wiping away tears and blowing her nose with tissues taken from a box on the table near her chair. She gave a half-hearted chuckle. "It's a good thing you have this perpetual supply here, Dr. Strictland."

"You haven't had to use them often, Eloise." Her smile was reassuring.

"No, but often enough," Eloise answered, wondering if Dr. Strictland kept notes on exactly how many times she had used tissues. She stood, saying, "Then, please go ahead, set up the appointments. I'll be there, but please don't tell my husband. He wouldn't understand at all." She snatched a couple more tissues from the box.

"Of course not. I would never reveal anything we've talked about." Dr. Strictland walked her to the door, opened it and held it for her. "For the time being, why don't I see you next week at the same time, and call me tomorrow after three. I'll let you know what I've found out." Eloise nodded and left, still wiping her eyes and nose.

Over the next two weeks, she juggled her schedule to make room for her added appointments, her first with Dr. Bennett, a bald-headed, portly man of fifty or so, who had interpreted the C/T scan she'd had the previous day. He'd found nothing, actually showing her the films, fuzzy prints of her brain that she could only gape at and that only he understood. She chose to believe that he was sincere and meant it when he said that she was in good health.

The psychologist that Dr. Strictland had her see, Dr. Green, aging, tall, thin and bewhiskered, said in a deep brogue, "Well, Mrs. Hamilton." They sat together in his small cluttered office. "You appear to be right as rain. I can find nothing to indicate a problem, except perhaps that you have too many irons in the fire."

She took his cute little colloquialisms to mean that she was in good health.

"Take a couple of weeks off from work," Dr. Strictland advised during Eloise's next appointment. "As I said before, I believe you're overly tired. Your family requires a great deal of attention. Your job is extremely taxing. Bottom line, you need a good rest."

No, she thought, she did not need a good rest, at least not for the reasons Dr. Strictland was suggesting. It didn't matter how many kinds of tests she was given or how much advice she received. She had seen what she had seen. She'd find out what was going on herself, and to hell with them all. She had thanked the well-meaning doctors who had worked with her. To Dr. Strictland she said, "I appreciate all your help, Dr. Strictland, but I won't be returning after today."

Eloise observed that Dr. Strictland rarely, if ever, displayed emotion, always remaining on a seemingly even keel. This time, however, her eyes registered surprise. "Do you think this is a wise decision to be making at this time?" She leaned slightly forward in her chair, further indication that she believed Eloise to be making a very grave error.

"I do," Eloise answered determinedly. "I believe I'm quite ready to handle things on my own now." She stood firmly and slung her purse over her shoulder.

Dr. Strictland rose with her, stating, "You first came to me because you had concerns regarding your marriage, then later, your job. It hasn't sounded to me," she said, "as though you've reached the point to where you're quite comfortable with things as they are."

"I am." Eloise smiled, but it was incomplete as she lied to herself and felt her stomach tighten.

Ritualistically, Dr. Strictland walked her to the door and opened it. "Call me if you change your mind."

"I will," Eloise promised, knowing she'd never call this woman again. As good as Dr. Strictland was, and she was one of the best, she hadn't believed Eloise.

Chapter Four

Bob was on top of her, and she was squirming around, trying like hell to get into it with him, but her mind was so busy it was impossible. He didn't seem to notice that she was dry or that he was hurting her. She endured her discomfort and continued her act. In a few moments, he fell exhausted to his side, and in seconds, he was out. She wasn't.

She lay wide awake staring into the darkness, carefully going over in her mind all that had happened the morning she had seen her most recent vision. Something had triggered it, but what?

She got up and slipped into her bathrobe and slippers. Downstairs in the living room she turned on a small, gooseneck lamp sitting on a tiny roll-top desk at which she paid the household bills.

Sitting down, she pulled out several sheets of stationery from a cubbyhole and began jotting down every bit of information she could recall regarding that first day she'd seen Tomstown and the children. In as explicit detail as she could remember, she described the weather, what she thought she might have eaten that morning, what she knew she had worn, the odor of baking bread and her inter-actions with the girls, how they looked, what they wore, the game they'd played, other people she'd seen and what they were doing. She included the fall that struck her unconscious. She covered con-versations with her grandparents and what she did for the remainder of her vacation with them. She also mentioned how she had felt toward the little girl, Marian Jones, whose name she'd never forgot-ten. She even redrew the rough sketch of Marian she had made on the margin of the newspaper a few weeks ago. She went on to write of her more recent encounter with the village and the women, filling several sheets, front and back. Meticulously, she compared the two entries. The single common bond seemed to be the smell of baking bread. But it hadn't been she who was doing the baking. The smell was already present, both when she was a child and these last times. She supposed she could try baking bread herself to see if that did anything.

She read and reread her notes, adding more details, more conver-sations. Bob had bought the kids a set of *Encyclopedia Britannica*. They sat on a shelf in the living room and were occasionally used by everyone in the house. She was grateful they had a set. It would save her going to the library as often as she might otherwise be forced to do, looking for facts.

She prowled through a variety of volumes, searching for any information regarding Tomstown. As she expected, there was none, but she learned a lot about the colonists war with England.

At five A.M. she had such a headache she had to stop and return to bed. In an hour she had to get up. For sure, she'd have bags under her eyes. Well, a little Avon would fix that right up.

She rose and stretched, then returned the Britannica volumes to the shelf and stuffed her notes in her pocket, somehow not comfortable with leaving them lying around. If Bob or the kids read them, they'd ask questions, and frankly, she had no answers.

Easter vacation had come and gone. The Mohawk scared a lot of people as it went through another historical flood. School was drawing to a close. Another month and summer vacation would be here. The kids were antsy and ecstatic. Caroline would be a senior and Bobby, a freshman. Eloise found their enthusiasm grating at times and their arrogance overbearing, but she assumed, and rightly so according to other parents with whom she'd spoken at work, that their children were also going through the "I'm moving up in the world, and I know it all" stage, and so she kept still.

Bob was at work much of the time, putting in twelve- and fifteen-hour days now that summer was approaching. After the long, cold winter and an exceptionally wet but warm spring, house-hunters were much more inclined to part with their money.

Since writing of her experiences, Eloise began baking loaves of bread. She tried every recipe she could lay her hands on, especially the ones that might have come from the 1700s, which looked to be the time in which the phantom town existed.

Evenings and weekends she attempted recipes she found at the library, and those from friends and an old recipe book of her grandmother's mother, endeavoring to recreate the aroma she'd detected during her "sightings," as she had come to think of them. She bought a couple of bread machines and several metal and glass bread pans and even a couple made of stoneware. The house frequently smelled of baking bread as she tried two or three different approaches. She placed containers of bread to cool on the kitchen windowsill and sneaked a couple of pans out to the field, leaving them where she thought she and the girls had played. At any given time there were one or two tins cooling on racks on the stove or kitchen counter. Her efforts did not bring back any sightings.

47

The sink piled high with dishes and flour plastered the front of her apron as her hands worked the dough before putting it into baking vessels, letting it rise for three hours, then punching it down so that it would rise once more before baking. Truthfully, she loved the bread machine best because it did the tedious job of mixing and kneading the flour for her.

She pretended she was having one hell of a good time and was cheerful toward the kids and Bob. She let them believe that she had found something to do that she really loved and lightened her spirits. She ignored the blaring TV and more frequently made love with Bob so that he thought she was in continuous excellent moods. Truthfully, she was exhausted all the time because baking after work, and even more on weekends, sapped her energy. When she should have been napping after supper and going to bed at a decent hour, she was *working*.

Her family loved her new hobby, especially since Eloise insisted on doing her own cleanup. The kids and Bob devoured hot, thick slices of bread slathered with butter or jam; they took sandwiches to school or work for the first time in years, then feasted on bread as an afternoon snack.

After an all-out, two-week baking marathon, Eloise stopped cold. As hot as this May was, she had stuck to her task while constantly watching out the kitchen window and back door. All she managed to glean from her efforts was a lot of wasted energy and too much bread, some of which she froze and some of which molded in the fridge or while stacked upon the counter. Her family just could not eat it all.

"But, geez, Mom, it's so good!" Bobby said. "Why'd you quit?"

"Look around you, kiddo," Eloise replied. She was peeling hard-boiled eggs. Supper would be light this evening; egg and olive sandwiches, pickles and chips, lime Jello and Cool Whip for dessert. The kids could drink whatever they wanted. She and Bob would have iced tea. Holding a half-peeled egg, she pointed. "Over on the shelf there are three loaves that died of gangrene today. This one—" She pointed again, at the table this time—"is still hanging in there."

"Well, you could bake more, couldn't ya?"

"I could, but I'm not going to. Supper will be ready soon, anyway, and we'll eat this loaf." She nodded at the bread near the freshly peeled eggs.

"But it might be moldy too."

"It isn't."

"You sure?" he demanded.

She smiled sweetly at him.

He looked disgusted as he retrieved his backpack from the table where he'd dumped it and went upstairs. She could hear him clomping all the way through the house and up to his room.

For the time being, it looked like the end of keeping the family ridiculously happy with fresh bread.

Caroline, however, was a surprise. She came downstairs after having changed her clothes from jeans and T-shirt to shorts and a tank top. It had been another 85-degree day. She walked over to the table and studied the bread. "Gone stale, I hear."

Eloise listened for hostility in her daughter's voice. There seemed to be none.

"There's more in the freezer," Eloise said, not looking up from her task, "but this loaf is fine, in case Bobby suggested otherwise."

"He said it had jungle rot."

Eloise chuckled. "Only his socks are guilty of that. Everything else in the house is safe."

For once Caroline laughed—lightly, but she was amused. "Well, Mom, I'm gonna miss the fresh bread, but it's getting pretty hot for baking anyway." She left the kitchen.

Eloise watched her beautiful daughter walk away. There was hope for Caroline yet. Moments later, rock music blared throughout the house, but she could stand it if, for once, Caroline was happy.

She heard Bobby return to the living room and flop down on the couch. Her children would be content until she called them for supper. With luck, they'd be content then too.

After supper, the kids borrowed her car and took off for the city softball games. She and Bob lounged on the back porch in two white wicker chairs placed on either side of a rusting TV tray. They sipped frosty glasses of mint iced tea. The old ladder-backed rocker, which Eloise's grandparents had once enjoyed, sat to one side, and she gazed upon it with love.

Bob asked, "Why'd you quit baking, honey? I thought you loved what you were doing."

"Got tired of it," she answered off-handedly. She could hardly give him the real reason. "Anyway, it's too hot anymore, and everybody's had enough. I've gained an extra pound, too."

"Me too," he said patting his abs.

"But it was fun," she countered.

No, it hadn't been fun. Not for one single minute. It had been a lot of sweat and exhaustion for nothing. All the while that she was baking, she'd kept meticulous notes on recipes used, times of day and night she'd baked, types of flour used—corn, bleached, enriched, stone ground, wheat, rye, oat, organic, inorganic; she noted whether she'd used the oven or bread-machine and if she'd baked in metal, glass or stone. She studied her data dozens of times looking for something, anything that might be a clue. She had learned nothing.

The following Saturday morning, she and Bob relaxed on the porch enjoying toast and coffee, and basking in the sparkling morning's sun. She crossed her legs and let a slipper fall from her foot. Her robe fell away from her legs. The sun felt like warm, caressing fingers stroking her skin. She closed her eyes and tipped her face to catch the heat upon her throat.

Bob rocked back in his chair. "How are you feeling these days, honey?" The kids were already out of the house for the day. Bob would go to the office only briefly, expecting to close a sale in downtown Herkimer, but for the moment they were peacefully alone.

His unexpected question jarred her. "I'm fine. Why?" She looked at him suspiciously.

"You seem a bit preoccupied," he said. "All this baking you were doing for the past couple of weeks. But what about the writing? What is it you're writing?"

She sighed as if the baking had been quite tedious and said, "I just needed to keep a few notes to remember what I'd done, but I'm bored with it now, I can tell you." And wasn't that the truth? If she never saw another baking tin, it'd be way too soon for her.

"Looks like a couple of books' worth to me," he said. Thinking that a couple of notebooks filled with recipes and other related information couldn't be too damaging, she'd left them on the kitchen table. It was, after all, just bread recipes. "What did you mean," he asked, "where you wrote, 'Nothing so far. Odor failing. No sightings'?"

Pasting a bright smile on her face, she asked, "Did I write that?" Yes, she had, and had forgotten. "Well," she said, carefully selecting her words. "Just a little creativity on my part. I thought," she went on, tapping a finger against her chin, "that if I could create not only a good-tasting slice of bread, but one that would also give off a pleasant enough smell to remind people of when their mothers or grandmothers baked . . ." Her smile extended into a giggle. "I guess I was taking it all a little too seriously, wasn't I? Every loaf of bread smells wonderful, even if the loaf collapses and turns out to be as heavy as a brick."

"Of course." Bob, quietly slurping, went back to gazing across the meadow. Eloise returned to nibbling toast, now nearly choking on every bite.

Bob stood. "Well, I'm off for the morning. Should be back by two at the latest. Want to do anything special?" He slipped into his suit coat.

Eloise gave his question some thought. "I'll think of something by the time you get back," she said. "Maybe a picnic over by the stream. We can dangle our feet in the water if it isn't too cold."

"I was thinking along the line of a movie."

The suggestion didn't excite her, but it was a better choice than debating the pros and cons of a pleasant walk outdoors versus statically sitting inside a darkened building and breathing everybody else's air for two hours or more on a gorgeous day like this. "Okay," she said without hesitation. "I'll find us a good one."

"Thanks, hon. You always do." He pecked her on the cheek and left.

As soon as he was gone, Eloise immediately retrieved the recipe journals and stuck them in the drawer where she kept all her notes. Retrieving her other journals, she settled down on the couch, her knees tucked beneath her. The beagles leaped up beside her and rested heavily against her legs as she leaned against the arm of the divan. She breathed deeply several times before reviewing all that she had thus far written.

She scanned the chronicle that listed the clothing she'd worn during her second sighting: her old terry bathrobe, which was radically different than that of the first sighting when she was nine and dressed in authentic period garb. Further, that outfit had been created on a treadle sewing machine. Should she take into account that no electricity had been used and no synthetic fabrics involved? Tapping her chin with a finger, she tossed around the thought for a while, then reread her notes. The robe was cotton, but parts of her slippers were plastic. Her wedding ring was gold.

Further perusal reminded her that she had opened the kitchen window to reach out and feel the sun's warmth. "Which hand?" she asked aloud. Her right. "That's it!"

She jumped up. Her heart began to beat furiously, and her hands shook so badly that she could barely insert the key into the lock after putting away the journals and then tugging on the drawer four or five times. There was no way on earth that she was going to leave anything lying around again no matter how innocent it appeared. Even if Bob and the kids were going to be gone for the next three years she wouldn't take the chance.

She gave the drawer handle one more solid tug, assuring herself that the journals were indeed safely locked away. Standing on a chair, she slipped the key behind a stack of dishes on the highest shelf in the kitchen cupboard.

Breathing deeply, she returned to the sink. Earlier this morning she had cranked the windows wide open. The dual windows didn't have screens. Bob would install them over the weekend. She extended her right hand. Nothing changed; she was disappointed. Her heart stopped pounding.

"Damn," she said, leaning hard against the sink, staring at the empty field beyond. She was so disappointed that tears blurred her vision. Then suddenly the town lay before her. Not fifty yards from the house, two women were staring straight at her.

Too startled to move, she remained immobile for several seconds while her mind grasped its only option: *Get your hand out of there and run like hell!* But run from what? And to where? What she was looking at wasn't real. All right, she was back to thinking that maybe this town could be real. But looking at it still scared the bejesus out of her. Slowly, she withdrew her hand, readying herself for a fast retreat. The moment her fingertips passed the sill, the scene began to fade. A guttural sound escaped her lips. Marian Jones belonged to that town. The woman for whom Eloise was enduring terrible agonies and deceits and loss of sleep.

Gritting her teeth, she was unable or unwilling to allow the disappearance of the town, and biting her tongue until she tasted blood, she reinserted her hand through the window, hoping that gesture was what had brought forth the image to begin with. Yes, the scene was returning. Resolutely, she pushed herself to keep her hand extended.

Statue-like, she examined the women watching her, recognizing the taller of the two, the one with the cleft chin—and a crooked tooth. She was the one Eloise spent so much time thinking about. "This," she whispered in a trembling voice while her knees turned to jelly, "is why I've gone through this. To see her. I wanted to see *her*."

Marian and her companion continued glancing her way as they chatted. Were they discussing her? Could they actually see her too? Timidly, Eloise waved, a tiny gesture that no one could have discerned at that distance. Trying to feel braver, she waved with more vigor. Both women smiled, returning her hello with hearty waves.

The next thing Eloise knew, she was lying on the couch, and Bob was sitting by her side.

Chapter Five

"I've called the ambulance. It's on its way." Bob placed a damp dishcloth on her forehead. She yanked it away from him and threw it to the floor.

"Get that filthy thing off me." A siren screamed in the distance as she struggled to sit upright.

Bob's hands on her shoulders gently restrained her. "Lie down, honey. You've had a bad fall."

"How would you know?" she asked angrily. "You weren't here."

"I found you in a heap on the kitchen floor with the beagles licking your face. That's how I know. Now lie down." He was insistent, bullying, certainly concerned. "What happened, anyway?"

"I slipped," she said. "I'm fine. Cancel the medics." She lay back and closed her eyes, listening to him sighing angrily and impatiently. Opening her eyes, she watched his jaw muscles clinching and releasing as he stared down at her.

Oh, God, why did he displease her so these days? He was a good man, a good provider and a good lover. He took care of them all, including his children and the dogs. She felt ashamed for rejecting his attempts to help her, but she did not need an ambulance.

Sighing, she said, "I'm sorry, honey. It's my period, I'm sure of it. I think I'm beginning my change of life." With enormous effort, she chuckled. "It messes with women's heads sometimes."

"I guess," he answered doubtfully. "You'd better see somebody, then."

The ambulance pulled into the driveway. Eloise sat up slowly, feeling slightly dizzy and nauseous. "I'm fine, Bob. Tell them I'm sorry for troubling them." He looked skeptical. "Go tell them, honey. Maybe I'll take a nap in a little while, and I'll see the gynecologist as soon as possible."

Reluctantly, he left her. She could hear him apologizing to the EMTs, the door closing, and then his returning footsteps.

"Maybe we should skip the movie this afternoon," he said, sitting precariously on the edge of the couch. She leaned against him as he put his arm around her.

"That might be best." She rubbed her arms with her hands, then glanced at the wall clock. "It's only ten-thirty. What happened? Fast sale, or no sale?" Thank God he hadn't arrived any sooner.

"Neither. The guy called and canceled."

"I'm sorry."

"He'll be back. His wife wants the house. I don't think he can stand up to her."

"How do you know that?"

"I saw her in action when I first showed them the place. She's a real pushy broad."

Eloise winced. "I wish you wouldn't call women that."

He released her and stood impatiently. "Some are. There's just no other word for them."

"How about just using 'woman.' Pushy woman."

"Doesn't sound as powerful. 'Broad' says it."

"To the uneducated, I suppose it would," she said tiredly. This whole conversation could turn into a nasty disagreement, but she was unable to let it go. Her dizziness was lessening, and for a change she was willing to argue.

"I'm hardly uneducated," he said, shifting his body weight just enough to let her know she had gotten to him.

"If I didn't know you, Bob, sometimes I wouldn't be able to tell. And I wouldn't like you." No, she couldn't let it go, but if need be, she was prepared to regret it.

"Too late for that, isn't it?" Playfully he chucked her under the chin with a finger. "I'm going to change my clothes, and then I think I'll wash the car. You rest. Take a nap like you promised."

She had promised no such thing. It had been a suggestion only. As she knew he would, he left her feeling as though she had lost yet another argument.

Not moving from the couch, she tried dozing a little, but it was impossible. How the hell was she expected to sleep when she had just greeted a couple of people who'd lived what looked to be about two hundred years ago?

Moments later Bob chugged down the stairs and rattled around in the kitchen, pawing beneath the sink for rags and a bucket. The screen door soon slammed shut.

Eloise breathed a sigh of relief that he was out of the house. She hadn't realized until that moment that she had been as tense as a violin string. She let herself go, feeling as though she were sinking through the cushions. Alone for a while, she could concentrate on what triggered the antiquated panorama, and how she might improve her ability to communicate with the women. She drifted off thinking about buying or making clothes.

"You asked me what I'd like to do. This is what I'd like to do."

Bob shook his head in amused dismay. "Next time I'll be more careful about what I say."

57

Eloise laughed lightly. "You'll enjoy it. Come on." Bob followed. They got into the car and headed for Herkimer.

"I won't enjoy it," Bob said as he pulled out onto the main highway. "I hate antiques. I thought you did too." He hunkered over the wheel like a truck driver about to begin a long, arduous trip.

"Oh, relax. We won't be that long. We'll hurry through the museum and then only take in a couple of shops. We won't stay long, and then we could have dinner." Eloise pulled down the visor to decrease the blazing sunlight bouncing off the car ahead.

"Then I'm having lobster Newburg," Bob pronounced. White-knuckled hands gripped the wheel.

"You'll be sick later. You always are."

"It'll be worth it," he retorted. "Antiques on a day like today," he said, ruefully shaking his head.

"You like some antiques. You know you do."

"Very few."

She let him stew and gave way to her thoughts. She was hoping against hope to find any kind of authentic period costumes of the 1700s in the shops and possibly buy a piece or two. Even if it were her wonderful fortune to stumble upon such treasure, she doubted she would be able to squeeze into them whatever size they might be. Better diet, nutrition and living styles, she knew, had enlarged overall human dimensions since then. At that time women were "dolls" and the men not much larger.

It was a fifty-minute drive to Herkimer. Bob flipped on the radio and searched for the public broadcasting station tuning into classical music. Adjusting the volume upward, he began humming to the energetic strains of Mozart.

They parked near the museum located in a vacated three-story, red-brick schoolhouse built in the 1940s. After paying a nominal admission fee, they wandered inside.

On the first floor were the eye-catchers. The museum leaned heavily toward the Colonial era. Full-sized male and female mannequins, including children, were displayed in period dress. Their bodies were small, a reflection of the actual sizes of people of that time. A number of weapons filled an entire wall: French muskets, American long rifles, knives with bone handles, tomahawks of stone and wood, bows and arrows galore. Glass cases held bullets, some with teeth marks in them from soldiers biting them while surgeons performed their duties without anesthesia. In the middle of the floor, a small cannon sat before a pyramid of several cannon balls welded together. Literature abounded; it would take a half-day just to read it all.

On the second floor were paintings, period furniture and dishes. Catching her eye was a large oil depicting General Herkimer and his men marching toward Oriskany. Smiling women, laughing children and leaping dogs followed the army. The background was of a country scene with cows grazing on gentle, rolling green pastures. The second painting was an enlarged replica of Frederick Yohn's famous painting presently housed in Cooperstown's museum, of Herkimer's fatal wound. The general rested against a tree, cared for by one soldier and surrounded by his army shooting at the enemy. Wrapped around his left leg was a bloody bandage. Herkimer pointed toward some distant place, consternation plainly showing on his face and that of all the men.

There were other paintings of the American Revolution, of life in general and of primitive home life in a cabin. Eloise carefully studied each scene, absorbing the details and reading as much as she could in the time she had. She lingered in the museum until she suspected that Bob had stayed his limit.

"Come on," she said. "Let's go look in some antique shops."

His eyes flickered only slightly as he nodded with tightened lips.

They visited three shops, staying not long in any, but Eloise had learned what she wanted to know. Bob was practically dragging himself along behind her. He kept picking up small items, then setting them down with obvious disinterest. She wound her way through narrow aisles of precious historical items interspersed with a lot of just plain junk. She pushed aside her growing sense of discomfort, which was triggered by Bob's bored sighs, and concentrated only on why she was here. Her gaze slid past bushel baskets of old canning jars, some in mint condition and others bruised. Long tables held cloth-bodied, ceramic-headed dolls in aging clothing, strange-looking tools and gadgets that only the old-timers would be able to identify, trays of unmatched silver, stacks of dishware, assorted lamps, picture frames and postcards. There was an array of other countless gadgets, goods and furniture, but she focused only on old clothing.

In two different shops she spotted two sizable quilts for sale, an 1823 with a wedding ring design and an 1879 of random colored blocks. They weren't from the 1700s, but she was certain there was no plastic or nylon thread involved in their making. A bit tattered though they were, they were still pricey but, she felt, manageable. There was also an old lace shawl and a lady's slip in one of the stores. She had seen no dresses. No matter. Hawk-like, she had studied the apparel of those women in the dioramas at the museum. She could draw a clothing pattern cold, if not well.

"Let's go, Eloise." Bob could stand it no longer. She sensed that his tenacity had been stretched to the limit.

"All right," she said cheerily. "I've had enough too. This place is gloomy."

"Damn depressing is what it is," he said, practically herding her out of the store and onto the bright sunny street. "How about something to eat?"

"Then a movie?" she asked.

"Sounds good." He took her arm as though he thought she might change her mind and return to the store or perhaps start searching for another shop. "There's a nice restaurant right around the corner. I think they have lobster Newburg there."

He still wanted seafood. She knew then how truly bored he was. She regretted his unhappiness and that she would probably be up with him half the night while he hung over the toilet tossing up an expensive dinner, but it was worth it to her. At the first opportunity she'd be back to pick up the quilts. The clothing she'd seen was just too small.

Chapter Six

Memorial Day weekend had been hot, and June was starting out that way as well. Sweat coursed down her face and trickled along her ribs. She had lied; oh, how she'd lied—to Bob and to the kids. She wasn't sick, not at all, but she needed today. She *needed* it.

She pressed her robe against her ribs to sop up the perspiration. She was scared, so scared that she thought she might die within the next few minutes. Or maybe this was the end of the world as she knew it, and she would never see it again and yet still be alive. She prayed, begging for guidance, for forgiveness for all her past transgressions and faults.

Except for her and the beagles, the house was empty. The noisy familiar slamming of cupboards, the kitchen's squeaking screen door, the closing car door, the rumbling bus had all died away. Bob's newspaper lay neatly folded alongside his dishes. Bowls of cereal sat about. Platters and silver were piled haphazardly in the sink and on the counter. Clutter prevailed.

After everyone cleared out and the hullabaloo had died down, Eloise straightened the house in record time. Following that, she went to her bedroom, dug deep down in the cedar chest where she had hidden the two frail quilts after having returned to Herkimer to buy them after work one day. The items had set her back a pretty penny. Bob certainly needn't know anything about it. She had her personal savings account. Carefully, she retrieved the precious possessions, then returned to the kitchen and placed the comforters on the table.

For twenty minutes she sat and stared at the quilts' patterns. She caressed the fabric, rethinking her plan to strip down to her skin, wrap the quilts around her body and step outside. What would happen if she did? Would the village be there? Could she talk to people? *Would she be able to return to her own time?* She couldn't imagine such a disastrous fate as becoming stranded there.

Placing one palm flat upon the material, she rested her head against her other hand and listened to her gurgling stomach as it churned honey-flavored Cheerios and black coffee into a vile, repugnant mass.

Bolting for the first-floor bathroom, she made it in time, just as her bowels exploded, doubling her over with vicious cramps. Gasping with pain, she drew the wastebasket between her knees and vomited. Great oceanic waves of nausea passed through her. She gagged until her eyes threatened to pop from their sockets; tears coursed like engorged rivers down her cheeks. Eventually the spasms subsided. She set aside the basket immediately, wishing she hadn't leaned over as lightheadedness attacked her. To counteract the appalling sensation, she rested against the back of the toilet, tilting her head back as far as she dared. She dreaded fainting in the bathroom. It would be so utterly undignified. She wondered at such absurd thoughts when she could barely maintain her equilibrium, but she was willing to entertain any bizarre notion if it would help deter her mind from how she was feeling just now.

Gradually her multiple discomforts eased, then ceased altogether, leaving her with a heady sensation of bodily weightlessness and sacrosanct relief that it was over, at least for the moment. At the sink, she washed her face with cool water, sloshed several handfuls over her head before toweling off, then brushed her teeth.

In the kitchen again, she avoided the table and instead stood gripping the edge of the sink and gazing through the casement window. She craned forward for a better look. Miraculously, suddenly the town materialized, alive and active. Adults and children moved about the village; dogs voiced their varied opinions. The weather was the same there as here, she could tell. The forest beyond the town was the same. After her two previous sightings, she had noticed that some of the trees, the bigger, older ones, were still the same, minus some of the larger branches and a number of burls that had grown on a few of the ancient trunks. It was a wonder that they still stood, that they hadn't long ago been cut down for a building or firewood.

She stuck her hands in her pockets and wondered why this scene had appeared just as she leaned against the sink. Something stabbed her left ring finger; quickly she withdrew her hand. A small piece of rusted metal protruded from her knuckle.

"Damn!" she barked. Squinting, she pulled the piece from her flesh and examined it. "Why, it's a piece of that old nail." she said to no one. Her next thought was the danger of tetanus. No, that wouldn't happen. Her shot was up to date.

She looked from the nail to the window. The village and all of its inhabitants were gone.

She glanced again from the insignificant piece of iron to the window as her mind whirled with possibilities. Very carefully, she set the nail on the counter and leaned against the sink. Nothing. She then picked up the nail remnant and again leaned against the sink. The town reappeared. People were still busy, carrying on with whatever they had been doing moments ago. Time was passing for them, just as it was for her. Those little girls she had played with were now grown women; the town had expanded by a few buildings. The forest was fuller and the trees taller than when she saw them in her own time.

Her own time.

She couldn't even contemplate her own time. Her time was now. Right now. But . . . so was the village's.

She was deranged. She knew it. Even with being checked out by all those doctors, she was a schizo, and they hadn't been able to tell.

"No, I'm not!" she hissed. "Those people are real. As real as I am." She watched a few minutes more. She was deathly afraid that Bob might appear, or the kids. Or anybody. Reluctantly, she put the nail remnant on the counter. The ancient scene dissolved before her eyes.

She set the bit of iron on the table and sat staring at it for a long, long time. She thought she'd thrown it out along with all the other junk that day she'd cleaned out her jewelry box and closet. This sliver must have gotten stuck in the terry cloth of her pocket. It was an enormous stroke of luck, enough to use up any and all other good fortune to which she might be entitled for the remainder of her life.

Her gaze again rested on the quilts, and again she began feeling sick as a dog. If it weren't for . . . for that woman . . . who was such a wonderful playmate for not more than half an hour two hundred years ago, she'd stop this whole moronic plan right now. If anyone ever found her out they'd have her on the psych ward so fast she'd think that Scotty had beamed her there.

She longed to talk to somebody, anybody, about this . . . this . . . She didn't even know what to call it.

She'd sneaked around, spent a lot money on things she shouldn't have, and lied. Oh, God, she'd lied to Bob and to the kids about being sick today, but maybe that part was no longer a lie, at least not the way she was feeling right now.

64

She sat up straight and looked toward the window over the sink. A warm breeze filtered into the kitchen. As far as she was from the town, she could tell that women were baking.

Women!

As though they were real. As though she knew them, and they her. As though she and they had a common bond—that of baking bread. She moaned in terror and rested her head against the shawl.

It took her another fifteen minutes to decide to go through with her intentions and another quarter-hour to actually disrobe. "Please, God," she whispered as she draped the bathrobe over the chair, "don't let anybody come home right now."

Trembling, she eyed the quilts. Maybe once wrapped in them and outside, she would just up and disappear and be nowhere at all. Possibly she would see nothing—or everything.

And *maybe she would see Marian.*

That was the thought that impelled her. Perhaps seeing her wouldn't be all that would happen. She might even talk with Marian and Agnes. After all, hadn't they already waved and spoken to her? At least that's what she *thought* had happened. And hadn't that caused her to drop in her tracks that day when they'd returned her wave? Well, by God, she wouldn't faint today. She couldn't! Who knew what would happen to her if she did? Where would she be? In her world? In theirs? In limbo?

Waves of panic washed over her. "What a wimp!" she snarled as she stood naked before the quilts awaiting her on the table. "Not me!" She tossed the blankets around her body and picked up the nail remnant. As she did the odor of baking bread became so strong, it was nearly disagreeable. "Fuck it!" she screamed and pushed open the screen door.

Chapter Seven

In the event that she needed to instantly retreat, Eloise parked herself just outside the door and clung to the knob. From here she couldn't see a thing. She'd have to leave the porch to see the field and town off to the right. Releasing her death grip on the knob, she stepped down and rounded the corner of the house. It was with great relief that she saw nothing but the big, empty field and the barn's old deteriorating foundation. She returned to the porch and dragged a wicker chair over to where she'd been standing. Seated, she let her wraps slip from her shoulders. It was a delicious feeling to let the sun seep into her bare skin. Its warmth soothed her as though she were being massaged by gentle fingers coated with balmy, exotic oils. A pleasant smell of baking bread wafted over her.

Suddenly, a fierce toothache struck her left canine. The pain was excruciating, and she grabbed her jaw with both hands. She must have jammed something between the gum and tooth. Her tongue searched the painful area. A throbbing set in, intensifying the discomfort with each passing second until she wanted to rip the tooth from her mouth. Her earlobes hurt, and now her fingernails ached as though burning slivers of bamboo were being rammed beneath each nail. Through it all, she kept the bit of old metal pinched between two fingers. She must never, never lose it!

"Mrs. Bellwether!"

She leaped to her feet as she frantically pulled her wraps around her. There before her lay the whole town, pictured more clearly than she had ever before witnessed. And several yards away were the two familiar women openly staring at her. Marian and her companion stood on that ever-present path upon which they seemed to walk each time Eloise had seen them. They were gawking at her, obviously shocked at her appearance.

Again she heard the name called out in alarm. "Mrs. Bellwether! Are you all right?" Marian spoke directly to her. The women lifted their skirts and began to run in her direction.

Horror gripped her, holding her spellbound as the ladies advanced. A whimper escaped her lips, jarring her from her paralyzed state of mind. She yanked open the door and plunged inside, tripping on the quilts that dragged around her feet. She fell forward, reaching for a chair to break her fall. Both she and the chair crashed to the floor.

Too stunned to rise, she curled into a tight ball, seeking to protect herself from whatever might come next, listening for the squeaking of the door's hinges, a voice, a touch, something. While she lay there, the smell of baking bread diminished, and the pain in her jaw lessened until both were completely gone. Able to think again, she murmured, "And just who the hell is Mrs. Bellwether?"

When enough time had passed, she discerned that nothing more was going to happen. If those women could have entered the house, they would have by now. For whatever reason—scientific, time-warp, spiritual—they were never going to come inside. She had a safe place, a fortress to which she could return if they ever came too near, for she already knew that she would again try to enter their world, and she still held tightly to the nail sliver, thank God.

She picked herself up and pulled on her robe, already planning how to make her next move. For starters, next time she would try with all she had in her to not run away. She might walk away—in a hurry—but she vowed never to run again.

She slept for a couple of hours, then began writing in her most recent journal. She had already filled three books cover to cover and was working her way through a fourth.

Once again, she described in meticulous detail the town as she had just seen it. At each sighting, the place stayed much the same; no major changes were taking place. The villagers always seemed to be the same people; Marian and her friend were always there. She detailed clothing, weather, the houses and outbuildings, yard gardens and what grew therein, given what she could see at that distance. It was her house that seemed to stand off by itself, surrounded by trees. She tapped the pen against her chin as she pondered why this place alone had been built so far from the village. An hour later she concluded her writing and locked away the journal.

After showering, she dressed in jeans, tank top and sandals, then headed out to the field. Here, in that other world, was a path upon which Marian and her companion always walked. She wondered if Marian stood there even now.

A sense of despondency and loneliness clobbered her as tears gushed from her eyes. Anguished cries broke the stillness of the sedate morning. She wrapped her arms around herself and swayed from side to side.

She felt silly but absolutely sane as she turned back to the house to strip to the skin, wrap herself in the quilts and retrieve the nail. Gallantly, she pulled herself together, ready once again to subject herself to this terror. She wanted to verify that Marian was really, really, *really* there.

This time she exited the house through the front door. She wished she could take a photo of the village but knew with dead certainty that she'd get nothing but an empty field. A camera was not of that world, but of this one.

Surprisingly, nothing happened. She saw no town, no people, no anything. There was only the usual view of field, McAdam Road out front, telephone poles marching alongside and looped with concave cable lines running from pole to pole and beaded with rows of noisy starlings. She withdrew and headed for the back door. As soon as she stepped outside, the aroma of baking bread besieged her. Instantly she was "there" and not "here." For whatever reason, exiting only through the screen door worked, which was the only door the women approached. Why would that be? Eloise wondered. The front door was much closer to their path than the back door.

Such a sense of elation struck her that she felt as though she were experiencing her first orgasm, an intimacy shared with her best girlfriend when they were seniors in high school. Even now she could feel her cheeks burning with shame as she thought of the incident, but her years-long guilt had never lessened the pleasure of that moment.

She put aside the memory, speculating on whether it would be possible to escape from her family whenever she needed a brief vacation from them. She thought it likely but also thought it possible that if they ever figured out her secret then they too could come here. This was assuming that what worked for her would work for them, and there was no telling what they would do in this culture. The concept was too appalling to consider.

Her plan was to remain out of sight, observing everything for as long as possible, to see if that other place—Tomstown—but more accurately Marian, stayed put.

Edging along the porch wall, she stepped down between the house and the thick, unkempt shrubbery that somehow never got pruned and now grew wild, some of the bushes growing taller than the windowsills. She dropped to her knees and crawled under the shrubbery. The ground was hard and stony, digging into her palms and knees. She rubbed tiny pebbles and sharp, poking organic matter from her flesh. The bushes caught at the quilts and dragged them from her back. She fought to keep herself covered, but after five minutes of struggling, she left the blankets where they lay and crawled on, naked as the day she was born.

She had maneuvered her way to the far edge of the house when again the toothache clobbered her. Simultaneously, her fingernails felt like searing blowtorches, as did her earlobes. Clutching her cheek, she buried a cry rising to her throat and waited for the blinding pain in her jaw to at least subside a degree so that she could go on. Instead, it increased to such a crescendo that she had no choice but to turn back.

On the way she retrieved the quilts. Despite the excruciating pain, she was exceedingly careful to protect the nail and keep the fabric away from the bushes. The quilts must not be destroyed. They were vital to her next step.

But first she needed to survive this one.

This time she didn't bother to redress but lay naked and gasping on the couch. In five minutes her toothache was completely gone, and her fingertips and earlobes no longer burned. She went to the desk and rapidly wrote in her journal, then called her dentist for his first available appointment.

Chapter Eight

"There is nothing wrong with your tooth, Eloise." Dr. Seymour's graying moustache bobbed up and down as he spoke. Highlights from fluorescent lights bounced off his balding pate. A white medical coat hung open and loose over his thin frame. Half-moon glasses perched on the end of his nose. He took a step back and righted the dental chair.

"That can't be," Eloise said. "It hurts like hell."

Clipped to the milky screen were her x-rays, taken moments ago by his hygienist. Dr. Seymour again peered at the films. Eloise watched his thick, wiry brows dance with concentration as he studied them. "I see nothing organically wrong, Eloise. That crown is fine, and unless I send you to a specialist, there's nothing more here in this office that I can recommend." He gave a small, apologetic shrug, returning the probe to the instrument tray.

He waited patiently while she considered this information. Something was going on here. Something didn't fit. "It's plastic, isn't it?" she asked.

"Well, not plastic, really. It's actually porcelain-covered gold."

"On a post."

"Yes, when we did the root canal, we put in a post and covered it with the crown." He pointed at the x-rays, showing her. "It looks exactly as it should as if it were real."

"What's it made of?"

"I told you," he said with slight impatience in his voice. "Porcelain over gold."

"Organic?"

"Yes, of course organic."

"How about the post?"

"Stainless steel. It's a good tooth, Eloise. Leave it alone."

"What's stainless steel made of?" she asked determinedly.

"Eloise . . ."

"What's in it?" she demanded.

"Well, chromium, nickel, other alloys that keep it from rusting. Why, Eloise, are you asking these questions?" His hands rested on his hips, his irritation with her evident.

"Chromium's organic," she said. "Was it used, say, one or two hundred years ago?"

He sighed. "I don't know. I doubt it. Certainly the average dentist didn't do more than pull bad teeth."

Her fingernails were painted with inorganic polish. Her earrings were just paste. Pretty, to be sure, but not real.

She spent several heart-wrenching seconds feeling sorry for herself, getting a firm grip on the idea that her porcelain-covered gold tooth, the only fake one in her head and the only one that had ever given her problems and that because of an old injury, and her fake fingernails and paste earrings, had to go.

"Can you replace the steel post with a gold one?" she asked.

"Yes."

"And put the old crown back on."

"If it isn't broken in the process, but to what purpose?"

"Because that's what I want. I'll pay you in cash. You won't even have to fool with insurance forms, but I want it changed!" Her eyes didn't waver as she spoke.

Dr. Seymour sighed, studying her. He put down his probe, then said, "Let my secretary set you up with an appointment with Dr. Mecenas. This is his field. He's an excellent man."

"Thank you."

Seymour leaned against the counter behind him, rubbing a hand over his face and shaking his head. "Eloise, why do you want to do this thing? It's expensive and completely unnecessary."

Eloise regretted Dr. Seymour's unhappiness, but it was a must that she remove this alien element from her mouth. There would be no more fake anything in or on her person. As she thought about it, the only thing that didn't seem to be a problem was her wedding band. Perhaps because it was gold. She decided she would take no more chances even with her ring that hadn't as yet given her any trouble but was larger than a gold post would be. She would remove it as well when she went to "the past."

Appointments with the specialist were scheduled for the following two Mondays. She would pay cash from her savings account for the work. Seven hundred dollars ought to cover it—and nearly wipe out her savings. Bob must never know. He footed enough bills as it was—all of the kids' dental and doctor bills, most of their clothing, all of the mortgage. She took care of the groceries and household necessities, which usually ate up most of her paycheck. Still, she'd manage to save a little each month, but very little.

On her way home, she stopped at the Valley Barn Bookstore. A half-hour's search in the large, overstocked barn led her to several fairly old books regarding "days of yore." She bought them all and stowed them in the trunk of her car.

That night, standing in their bedroom, Bob held her close and stroked her hair. She had been exceptionally moody all evening. The kids avoided her by hiding in their rooms, and even Bob tiptoed around her. "I think you ought to have a checkup. See somebody, maybe your shrink, or a regular doctor. And your fainting spells . . . They worry me." He talked into her hair.

"There's nothing wrong with me, Bob." She freed herself from his embrace. "I'm just plain tired these days. Always hurrying here and hurrying there. I just need to slow down. Even Dr. Strictland said I work too hard."

"You don't need to work at all," Bob said. "I've told you that a million times." He pulled her back into his arms.

"But I want to." She yielded to him, wrapping her arms around his waist and resting her cheek against his chest. He felt strong and safe, and Dr. Strictland had said no such thing to her. She regretted this lie, too, and wondered why she had fabricated it. It hadn't been necessary.

"Then why not just take a couple of weeks off? Go visit Betty and Ray. Binghamton's not that long a drive."

That was some concession on his part. If there were two people Bob didn't care for, it was his in-laws. They had yet to approve of him, or he them.

"Or go see an old girlfriend," he said. "Go dig in the Herkimer Diamond Mines and visit General Herkimer's home, too. Hang around those musty old museums. I know you love to do that."

She heard the smile in his voice. He hated most everything old. If something broke, he replaced it with new. She would tinker for hours trying to repair something. Sometimes she was successful, sometimes not. The food blender still worked after twenty years of use, and so did the vacuum cleaner, although these days it was pretty well held together with duct tape and good luck and really should be replaced. She enjoyed frugality in some ways, but she also enjoyed new things: a few new gadgets for the kitchen from time to time, some new dresses or shoes—and paste earrings.

She'd been quiet for so long that he asked, "Would you consider a vacation, honey? For my peace of mind? In fact," he said magnanimously, "I wouldn't even expect you to fix my breakfast or bring me my morning paper if you stayed home while you took some time off. Lie in bed every morning if you like. I'll deal with the kids." And didn't that comment raise her eyebrows?

As newlyweds, she loved being the first to rise, making them both a big breakfast of homefries, bacon or sausage and eggs with toast. While coffee brewed, she retrieved the morning paper from the mailbox. Passing through the living room she would stop at the foot of the stairs and call out, "Breakfast is ready."

Within five minutes, Bob would be seated at the table, his breakfast before him, coffee poured, the paper by his plate. That was a long time ago. Over time he had come to expect it as his due. For her, it had taken all the fun out of their morning ritual; she had come to hate doing it. Unable to figure out how to tell him so, she had continued with what was now a tedious chore. And now, of course, there were the kids. At least she no longer fetched for them. When they had each reached the age of eight she told them to get their own breakfast as long as it was cold cereal. She thought she'd waited too long telling them even then and continued preparing their eggs and hot cereal until they were ten. Taking care of one baby for the rest of her life was enough for any woman.

"A vacation," she said.

"For two weeks—at least." She felt his deep voice vibrate in his breast and resonate in hers, felt his big heart beat against his chest and hers. "I know you've got vacation time coming."

She thought about it. "I don't think I've ever done that. Not for two weeks in a row."

"Then you should," he declared. "The kids and I will work around you. Caroline and Bobby usually stay at their friends' houses on the weekends anyway. It would probably be pretty quiet around here."

"The kids say they don't get nagged at their buddies'. That's why they like it there."

"Oh, all kids say that, Eloise. You know that. Besides, you don't nag them here." Bob began to pull her T-shirt over her head.

"I don't do anything with them," she said, raising her arms. Bob slipped off the shirt. He reached around her and unhooked her bra, letting it fall to the floor. "I should be down their throats over a million things. But I'm not." Her words saddened her. She preferred not to argue with the kids about their messy bedrooms with clothes strewn all over, or the bathroom with long strands of Caroline's hair clogging the sink and used bath towels tossed on the floor. Bobby avoided taking out the garbage or burning the papers in the burn-barrel. Then there was the housework that her daughter never seemed to have time for. "I hate arguing with them."

"Right," Bob said. He ran his hands over her shoulders and down her arms.

"Right," she agreed tiredly. Or with you, either, she wanted to add. And she silently asked him, Why don't you go get your own morning newspaper? You're the one who reads it.

She was quickly working herself into a dismal mood. She didn't want that. She wanted her husband to hold her and kiss her and tell her that everything was going to be all right. Unfortunately, his saying nothing implied that everything *was* all right.

She tried to adjust her temperament, saying, "You're probably right. I'll see about taking some time off, but I think I'd rather stay right here on the porch soaking up the sun and rocking the days away. It would be much more restful than driving all over the place."

"That's probably wise," he said. "Putter around here. Relax. It'd do you good to not move for a change. And like I promised, you won't have to cook a thing."

"I'll make supper," she said. "I don't want to feel like a guest in my own home."

He smiled and rested his hands on her breasts, squeezing gently.

She didn't feel anything, but she pretended to while her thoughts now focused on the freedom that would come with those two weeks, the research she could do, the clothing she could possibly make, the time she could spend watching the "other" place—Tomstown—and her dear friend, Marian.

Chapter Nine

Because the staff's summer vacation schedule was already set up, Eloise knew she'd have to pay a mighty high price to get anyone to change at this late date.

Meg, her best friend at work, would relinquish her week's vacation only if Eloise promised to attend her next three Tupperware parties whenever they happened. She gave Sally, whose vacation immediately followed Meg's, and who was not well-liked by her colleagues because of her annoying ways (toward the staff, not the patients), fifty dollars.

Putting the two weeks together was costly. Eloise hated Tupperware parties, and fifty dollars to that Sally was a very high price. But their supervisor agreed, and Eloise had been able to quickly accumulate a two-week vacation. She considered herself very clever.

She used her vacation judiciously. As soon as Bob left the house and the kids headed for school, and knowing what time to expect everybody home, she gathered her recently purchased books from the car, pulled her journals from the desk and parked herself on the back porch. Seated in her grandmother's rocker, she devoted her time to reading and writing notes regarding homemaking, crafts, health remedies, food preservation, herbs and their attributes. She looked into quilting, spinning, sewing and soap-making. After her second and last dentist appointment Monday afternoon, she haunted the antique shops and old barns of Ilion and Herkimer.

Tuesday morning, she searched through the Ilion library's many telephone books from surrounding cities and towns, searching for the Bellwether name. There were fifteen listed in Utica, and several more scattered in outlying towns and nearby counties. Apparently, Bellwether was an established personage in this region, but until she'd heard it from Marian's lips, the name had remained unknown to Eloise. Also, she learned nothing of Tomstown.

Early Wednesday morning she decided to drive to Cooperstown about an hour and a half from Frankfort Center. Cooperstown's rich early American history drew her. It was also home to renowned novelist James Fenimore Cooper, author of the *Leather-Stocking Tales* and Walter D. Edmonds, who wrote *Drums Along the Mohawk*, which popularized the area. She had been here before with Bob and the children, taking in the vastly popular Baseball Hall of Fame. It was the only thing they had seen that day, the trip being taken for the children's sake, especially Bobby's. This time she made a trip to steep herself in Cooperstown itself, devouring all that she could possibly absorb in her allotted time.

She spent time at Cooper's home, taking the forty-five-minute tour given by Mrs. Smith, a local historian. Eloise admired the old structure and its priceless antiques. Hearing how Mr. Cooper lived during these times made his life seem so simple, but then he was a fairly wealthy man.

At the Farmers' Museum, she plainly saw the intensive labor less fortunate men and women, and also the children, performed to carve out a living in this valley. They used horse- or ox-drawn plows on a daily basis. Tools made of iron, wood and leather included axes, augers, wood planes, drills, bores, mallets, differing hammers and dozens of others she couldn't name. Both animals and people wore yokes to haul things. A physically exhausting life, Eloise thought. There were no easy jobs. Even the spinners and weavers, she had learned, suffered from chronic backaches from sitting so long.

She lunched in town, first seeking out a McDonald's, but Cooperstown allowed no fast-food establishments within its city boundaries. She settled for a small cafe on the edge of Otsego Lake and watched the sailboats drift by on the wind while eating corn bread and beef stew.

Her journals piled up, and she took to hiding them in her grand-father's old metal toolbox, which she concealed downstairs in the cellar behind the door of the old root cellar. No one ever used this room. It was a small dark, dank place full of cobwebs and spiders. A few shelves were rotting and falling down. She positioned a nonde-script piece of decaying plywood over the box before pulling the door closed behind her.

She was extremely diligent about being home before Bob and the kids each evening, but during the day she scrambled, cramming in and completing each task scheduled for that day. Evenings, she and Bob rested on the porch sipping iced lemonade from frosty glasses or cold beer from sweating glass bottles while the kids lolled around watching TV or doing their homework. Mornings after breakfast, Bob came upstairs where she still lay in bed. She didn't rise until the house cleared and became so quiet that she could hear vehicles sail-ing down the main highway, two miles away.

The weekend went by quickly and pleasantly. The kids, it turned out, stayed home. She found she actually enjoyed her time with them and with Bob. They held a barbeque on the deck Saturday evening and Sunday afternoon, Bob, the kids, and she took in a movie together in Utica, an unheard of thing for this family for the last five years. Everybody seemed contented.

Today, Monday, began her second week of solitary vacation. That left her five more uninterrupted days to . . . to . . . Was she truly prepared for what she was about to do? Her musings frightened her. She bounced out of bed and took a quick, cold shower to break the pattern to which her mind was falling prey, that of obsessing on her upcoming ventures.

She dressed, hurried through a light breakfast, then cleared the table. On it, she spread out one of the antique quilts she'd retrieved from the cedar chest. It sickened her that she needed to destroy the comforters, but she must make period clothing, and this was the only material she had been able to find. Prowling through Herkimer's old shops last week had, in the end, yielded nothing else useful.

Using the plain backings of the quilts, she literally sweated away the next two overly warm days by picking away the old stitching to free the backing. There were thousands and thousands of stitches, and it was a tedious and boring job to remove them. From cutting, shaping, basting and frequent donning and removal of cloth slowly emerged a simple, plain wraparound skirt and, much more challenging, a blouse. She sewed with unmercerized white cotton thread purchased in a specialty sewing shop, asking to be certain that the fiber was free from this century's touch, other than having been machine spun. The sewing needles were made of steel.

Taking no chances, she had checked that steel needles were acceptable to use, by reading about them in the *Encyclopedia Britannica*. It listed China as having made the first steel sewing needles, which the Moors brought to Europe in 1370. That being fact, she felt safe using them, but before use, she doused them in rubbing alcohol to be sure there was no residue from prior handling. Apparently she could sew with steel; she just couldn't have any in her body. There had to be some foreign element in her tooth's steel post that was *not* okay. Thank God she'd never had any operations requiring *permanent* internal metal parts, like a hip joint.

Short on material, she'd worry later about making a cap and apron and only if not wearing them seemed odd to Marian and her friend.

As she worked, guilt weighed her down. She had said nothing to Bob about her sewing and concealed all evidence that she was. Wasn't that a lie? And the reason for making the clothing, to step into another world . . . Wasn't that deceptive as well? Yes, that was a biggie. Cleaning up and packing away her project at the end of each day was an enormous relief as she closed and sat resting on the cedar chest.

On Thursday, without interruptions, her wardrobe completed, she trembled as she dressed before the full-length mirror in the bathroom upstairs. The clothes seemed to be holding up well enough. At least they wouldn't fall apart when she moved, not if she were very careful. She wasn't planning on sneaking behind the shrubbery again. This time she would walk out the kitchen door, and if her knees didn't buckle, she'd stroll over to where Marian and her friend always seemed to be. If it was possible, and her heart hadn't given out by then, she'd even speak to them.

All right, then! It was time to go. She had on period clothing; a gold post had replaced the steel in her tooth which had healed nicely. Her nails were stripped of polish, her earlobes naked. She was barefoot, with no shoes yet found to be appropriate to her costume. She had showered with an all-natural bar of soap she'd picked up at a natural food store. She was ready. No! Not quite. Even though her wedding band hadn't bothered her at all, she still did not trust that the metal was free of foreign elements. Remembering the pain of those other times, she felt she must remove the ring. But she hadn't had it off since the day of her marriage. What would taking it off signify? *Nothing!* It would signify nothing at all. She loved Bob, her family, her present life. She only wanted to reintroduce herself to Marian—if she could. She *needed* to! Marian was her friend. Some friendships are made in an instant and last a lifetime. But whose lifetime, she wondered.

At the kitchen sink, she ran cold water over her left hand and the band came off, painfully pinching her knuckle on the way. Her hand shook as she carefully placed the ring in the middle of the table. A wide surface was the safest place for it. If she ever lost it, she'd never forgive herself. Neither would she ever be able to explain its loss to Bob.

"All right, Eloise," she said, still staring at the ring. "Either cook or get your ass out of the kitchen." Grabbing the old nail sliver from the desk and wrapping it in a scrap of quilt, she tucked it into a small, deep pocket of her skirt she had added at the last minute just for this purpose.

She breathed deeply, then slowly exhaled before advancing toward the screen door. The hinges squealed pleasantly as she exited the kitchen. Stepping off the porch, she looked toward the village and steeled herself for her future—or was it her past?

Ways to stall flew through her mind. Her clothing could fall apart when she started walking; she had no basket to hang over her arm; she didn't have a lace handkerchief to tuck into her sleeve. Her excuses became fewer and more ridiculous.

Another deep breath steadied her as she observed the village. There it stood as always. And there stood Marian and her friend on the path. Everything looked so normal.

She waited for something to happen—possibly another toothache, or perhaps she wasn't wearing the correct clothing or enough of it. After all, she was barefoot. How important was footwear right now? She patted her pocket feeling the lump of cloth that held the nail. It's small bulk comforted her.

The women had been talking to each other, but they stopped and looked her way. They seemed surprised to see her there as both gave her a wave.

Apparently Eloise was in good shape for the moment. Nothing hurt, she was still standing, still breathing. Now all she had to do was wave back and walk toward them.

And this she did.

Chapter Ten

Eloise's heart thundered arrhythmically, leaving her uncomfortably breathless. The June sun was blazing today. The smell of baking bread in the air was strong and almost nauseating. This dismayed and frightened her, and she took it as a bad sign. Of what, she couldn't say, but then what could she say about any of this?

The women appeared to be waiting for her. They watched her as she moved toward them. Five yards away from them, no one had yet spoken, but the ladies were smiling.

It was indeed Marian who stood before Eloise. There were great tears in her eyes; a slight smile kissed her lips. And there was that crooked tooth, Eloise noted, that Marian still had. Both ladies wore plain, wheat-colored linen blouses and blue skirts. Small caps were perched upon their heads, and both also wore braided hair wound about their heads. Over one arm, Marian, slightly taller than Agnes, carried a basket of bakeware protected with cheesecloth covering.

Eloise had figured it right when she made her own skirt and blouse, which were so close in design that they could have come directly from this time. The only difference was that she was barefoot and they wore leather shoes that were neither left nor right. That concept hadn't yet been born.

A yard's distance away, Eloise stopped before them, her head reeling and her skin clammy and cold in spite of the midday warmth. At her sides, her hands clutched and released her skirt as sweat coursed along the sides of her face and rolled down her neck and back. Beneath her armpits moisture soaked her blouse. Only the soles of her feet were cool as she stepped onto the grass beside the path.

What in *hell* was she doing here?

She should speak, say something, anything! She should take command. She was by far taller than them, twentieth century health standards and nutrition, Eloise knew, being contributing factors. She was educated beyond what these women could possibly comprehend, and yet they were the ones who seemed relaxed, knowledgeable, sure of themselves. But of course they would. They belonged here. She didn't!

She started to turn away, casting aside her earlier promise to herself that she would not run. To hell with that. She was leaving and not stopping before she hit the next county, maybe even the next state.

As she turned to flee, Marian reached out saying, "I'm so glad to see you, Eloise." She put a hand on Eloise's arm. "I'm so very, very glad," then drew Eloise into her arms. Large breasts pressed against Eloise's smaller ones. Marian's body heat penetrated Eloise's blouse; the smell of cloves were on her breath.

At Marian's touch, Eloise nearly screamed. Her breakfast leaped to her throat, but she fought the nausea, repeatedly swallowing until she was in control of at least her stomach.

Marian had substance, density, like that of a real body. She was real, as real as Eloise herself. She stood rigid in Marian's arms, her head tilted slightly back while Marian freely rested her cheek against

Eloise's chest, the basket still draped over Marian's arm poking her in the hip.

"Your heart is pounding so, Eloise, dear. I'm sorry you're so upset," Marian said.

Speaking warmly, Agnes added, "Don't worry, Eloise. You'll always have loved ones waiting for you, thinking of you, praying for you."

Praying? Why? But now wasn't the time to ask, and she couldn't continue standing there as stiff as a telephone pole with Marian holding her so tenderly. She raised her hand and placed it on Marian's shoulder. Her fear dropped away, her heartbeat returning so quickly to normal that she felt a slight stab of pain in her chest. Lord, not a heart attack now!

She ventured further, extending her arms around Marian's small shoulders and embracing her. She closed her eyes and expelled a deep, satisfied sigh.

Only once in her life had she ever experienced complete internal peace. It had been warm that spring evening back in 1958, much like the ones occurring these days. She had been on the porch occupying the same chair in which her grandparents had once rocked. That was the day she became owner of their estate. The house and land were now hers; beside her on a TV tray was the signed deed. She was sipping a vodka collins. Stars began to glisten. That night, they were brilliant. The peepers sang, tiny frogs no bigger than the end of her little finger and making as much noise, at a phenomenally higher pitch, as the bullfrogs would later make in the season with their deep bass croaking. The rocker pleasantly squeaked. In the house, all the lights had been turned off. From her chair, she scanned the barn in the faint moonlight, the field beyond and the woods farther out. Lightning bugs, which she called "earth-stars," filled the dark places. Peace engulfed her. All was right with her universe. Eventually, mosquitoes drove her inside, but for a little while, life was complete.

Now that same sensation came flooding back to her as she embraced Marian. She hadn't noticed until this second the lavender scent radiating from Marian's hair.

I love you, Marian. I've loved you since I was nine years old. I've never loved anyone else like this. Not even Bob.

"How are things going?" Marian asked softly. She still clung to Eloise.

How was she to answer that? Even in her struggle to find an appropriate response, her inner being remained peaceful and still. "What's being said?" she asked.

"I'm not one to say."

"Gossip is useless," Agnes said, "and unkind."

"Yes, that's true," Eloise agreed. She must tell them something. Still, she was tranquil. She stepped back from Marian, leaving her hands to linger on the smaller woman's shoulders. She looked into Marian's eyes. "What do you believe, Marian?"

"That you will speak about things if you wish. That you will not shame yourself."

"You saw me naked," Eloise said. "Is that not shameful?"

"No." Marian's eyes looked pained. "He's wrong. The whole village knows it."

"Marian, you're gossiping," her sister said in a sharp, scolding voice.

"Agnes, someone must defend her."

Agnes had changed a great deal since childhood. Her teeth were very bad. Her face was full of wrinkles. Osteoporosis was evident in her spine.

Agnes asked as her eyes registered fear, "Where's your husband?"

"He's gone for the day." At least that part was truthful.

"Hunting, I suppose," Agnes said.

Eloise avoided a direct reply. "I'm free today," she said. "I'd like to stroll through the town, if I may."

"Is that wise?" Marian asked. A jolt of fear shook Eloise. She hoped walking around in a time that occurred two centuries previous wouldn't outright kill her! "If your husband finds out . . ." Marian was saying. Her voice dropped, a look of unease in her eyes.

"I'm sure he'd have something to say if he knew what I was doing," Eloise answered honestly. "But he won't find out unless I tell him."

"There are gossips here," Agnes warned sharply. "Nasty old women. Terrible wagging tongues. As if they had nothing better to do with their time."

And a couple of hundred years from now, Eloise knew, those old women wouldn't have changed one iota. "They won't tell," Eloise assured them. A thought popped into her mind. They *would* tell. Not Bob, certainly, but somebody. Just who was her husband here? "But," she asked, "if they do tell, what do you suppose they'll say?" She looked pointedly at Agnes who seemed to have the inside scoop on the townsfolk's shortcomings.

Agnes flipped a casual hand. Her eyes rolled dramatically. "Oh, I'm sure they'll say something like, 'I saw Mrs. Bellwether in town today with the Allen and Whitehall sisters,' the old biddies." So the sisters had married, Eloise thought. "'Those two are going to get that woman in terrible trouble with Mr. Bellwether.' And their heads will bob in agreement like a flock of chickens pecking at the dirt."

Marian pursed her lips, nodding in agreement.

"Why do you think he acts so, Agnes?" Eloise questioned, believing Mr. Bellwether was her husband. She added a deliberate tinge of sadness to her voice. If she could just nail down his first name.

"You know I love you, Eloise," Agnes began.

"We both do," Marian added, looking deeply into Eloise's eyes. Her ardent gaze rattled Eloise to her bones.

Why are you looking at me like that, Marian?

She averted her eyes, saying cheerfully, "Of course you do."

"But . . ." Agnes seemed at a loss for words.

"We hear he's so terribly jealous," Marian finished. Her cheeks flushed. "I sound as bad as those old crones." She bowed her head, saying, "I'm sorry, Eloise. I had no right to speak."

"Some things can't be ignored," Eloise answered. It was a safe enough reply and could have been applied to almost any comment made.

"A fortnight ago when you came out of your house with . . . with . . ." Marian was nearly in tears.

"You mean with just the quilts covering me?" Eloise prayed that she and these women experienced the same event.

"Yes," Marian said. "I don't think anybody else saw, except Agnes and me. At least we haven't heard anything, have we, Agnes?"

"Not so far, sister."

How close the three of them seemed to be, right here in this world. Tiny thrills of pleasure darted through her chest. Not one man-made piece of debris orbited the Earth, she thought, or rested on the surface of the moon. Time and the Earth were as clean as when they had been created. She looked toward the heavens. White clouds floated against a blue sky with its ozone layer still intact. Birds flew about landing in trees and bushes and on the ground. Not one strand of wire sliced the air; there were no jet engine noises or vapors. If these only people knew what lay in their future, Eloise contemplated, they would not change a thing, now.

She looked toward the cluster of houses and shops; the scene was like a beautiful, tiny model village. In her time, one paid twenty dollars for a fine replica of one such building, all to recreate Christmas villages of old and display them on mantlepieces during the holiday season. Perhaps people longed to capture a bit of nostalgia that they would otherwise never experience.

"I'm thankful for that," she replied. She didn't need gossip-mongers just now.

"For him to have pushed you out the door like that with not a stitch on your back. So shameful." Agnes extracted a small block of tatted cotton from the pocket of her apron. That was another gift from Eloise's grandmother—teaching her how to tat. There were several tatted hankies and doilies in the cedar chest that she had made over the years. Agnes dabbed her eyes dry.

"We've pried enough," Marian said. She too wiped away tears using the sleeve of her blouse. "Why don't we just sit and chat here? It would cause less commotion, and the grass seems dry." Without waiting for a reply, she plopped down, straightening her skirt around her. She looked up, smiling, a virtual sunburst exploding across her face.

She glows from within, Eloise thought as she and Agnes joined her. And I suspect that she's afraid for me. As soon as possible Eloise would further research this Mr. Bellwether.

Though disappointed that she wouldn't be visiting Tomstown, she accepted Marian's judgment. There would be another time. At night, perhaps, when everyone was asleep, maybe during a full moon on a clear evening so that she wouldn't trip over something and kill herself while she was sneaking around. She'd have to be more cautious than a cat burglar. Just considering the idea scared her.

Agnes rested her arms across drawn knees. "I wondered if we would ever see you again, Eloise. What's it been? Near thirty years?"

"A long time," Eloise answered. She was talking to people who'd been dead for centuries. It frightened her in spite of their being warm, friendly and caring ghosts—if that was what they were. In Eloise's arms, Marian hadn't felt like an apparition. "I've missed you," she said, carefully avoiding the eyes of either woman. "More than I can say."

The sisters nodded. "Where did your ma and pa move to?" Marian asked. "We never did hear."

Oh, Christ, now she needed a history. What, *what*? "We moved over near Albany," she said.

"What's it like there?" Agnes asked. "I've never been much past Tomstown's limits."

Thank God, a simple query. Eloise picked a piece of grass and twirled it between her fingers. "It's much the same as here," she said. "Lots of trees, animals . . . Lots of houses."

"Any savages?" Agnes asked anxiously.

Yeah, but most of them are white.

"Call them Indians," Marian admonished. "You don't want people calling you a European or a foreigner, do you? Mama taught us better."

Agnes shrugged. "All right, then. Indians. But did you see any?"

"I don't recall seeing too many," Eloise answered. "Are there many here?" she asked.

"Some," Marian answered. They're pretty restless over on the Mohawk River . . ."

"It's flooding this year," Agnes added.

Yes, it is, Eloise thought. It was another fact that indicated their weather patterns were running simultaneously.

Marian continued, "But we been lucky so far. Oh, they come by begging and stealing from time to time. Otherwise they haven't been too bad."

Begging and stealing to survive, Eloise thought, a position into which they were forced by an encroaching white population. "Why is this place called Tomstown?" she asked.

"Somebody named Tom lived here first," Agnes answered. "That's all I know."

Eloise nodded. "Makes sense, I guess." It suddenly occurred to her that she was unbearably tired. She felt sluggish and muddled, suspecting that she was here on borrowed time, and needed to return to her house. She rose on unsteady feet. "I must go now," she said, trying to hide her discomfort. "Baking calls me."

Marian and Agnes looked blank.

"I need to do some baking," she said.

"Oh," they responded simultaneously.

Keep things real simple, Eloise reminded herself. "I'll come visit soon," she promised.

"Don't get yourself in trouble on our account," Marian warned as she stood and brushed herself off. Agnes picked a dandelion and handed it to Eloise.

"Thank you, Agnes," Eloise said, "and don't worry. I'll take care of . . ." She let the sentence hang, hoping that somebody would say Bellwether's first name. Her pause paid off.

"It isn't that I don't like Enos," Marian said. "It's just that he seems so . . . strict with you."

"Well," Eloise said magnanimously. "I love Enos, so don't worry. We'll work things out, I'm sure."

Both sisters looked doubtful. Marian reached out and tightly hugged Eloise. "I do hope so. I'd hate to see him acting so and then leaving you alone while he goes marching off to war."

"War?" Eloise frowned in confusion. *What war?*

"We'll beat the British back yet," vowed Agnes. "I'll fight them myself, if I have to."

"Oh, don't go getting on your high horse," Marian said, stepping back from Eloise. She frowned angrily at her sister. "You're always so ready to go to battle over any little thing. Just like Pa was, and you see where it got him!"

With her mind still on Marian's ever-so-brief mention of war, Eloise had to ask, "Where did it get him?"

"Buried up in Fort Ticonderoga on Lake George. Wasn't but twenty-one years old when he got himself killed. Me and Agnes never knew him. Ma, she said she just took the news like she expected it. She didn't find out about it until a year later. A soldier coming back from there told her."

Agnes spoke sharply, angrily. "Ma said Pa was a wandering man. Men are such fools."

"And your mother?"

"Ma worked herself to death raising us," Marian continued. "She died after we were both married. She always said she wanted to see her girls married before she went."

"She did, too," Agnes said. "The day after I got married. Marian was already married in fifty-three. She didn't waste any time living beyond that."

"Broken hearts can do that," Eloise said compassionately.

"My heart almost broke once," Marian said.

"How, Marian?" Eloise asked, feeling more ill by the minute but reluctant to leave.

"Not how so much as when," Marian answered. "When you moved away. It was hard for a long time afterward, for me. You had become such a good friend so quick. I came everyday to play with you, but you and your family left that night, Mama said. She said your pa was always a restless soul."

"Like they all were back then," Agnes added. "Always going west, always talking about going west, always dragging their families off to some awful place or other. We lost lots of friends that way, didn't we, Marian?"

"That we did, sister," Marian replied.

Eloise looked at them. "I missed you too," she said honestly. "And I'm so glad to see you again." She felt lightheaded. "But I really must go now or I'll never finish my baking in time."

"Of course," Marian said. "At least wave to us when you can."

"I will," Eloise said, already making her way back to the house. "You take care, Agnes. And don't go fighting with anybody."

"Ha!" Marian answered playfully. "She's thirty-nine years old and still as scrappy as a cur."

Agnes gave her sister a playful slap on the arm, and they started back down the path together, still calling out good-byes.

Eloise did her best to return their farewells, but it was a supreme effort even to raise her hand.

As soon as she hit the house she went to her bedroom, removed the fragmented nail from the skirt pocket, stuffing it into the farthest corner of the coffer, hid her clothing in the chest, then headed for a cold shower. The sensation of illness left her as the water beat down on her. Afterward, she dressed hurriedly and dashed downstairs to erase any telltale signs she may have left behind of her venture, including slipping on her wedding band.

Secure that everything was copacetic, she sat outside in the rocking chair to write. She would record everything she could while her memory was still fresh. Some thoughts chilled her. She didn't want to get mixed up in any war. Nor did she have to. Not if she never put on those old clothes and took the nail beyond the walls of her house again.

Thinking about it, she knew she wouldn't stay away. Not even the war would prevent her from seeing her friends again. Friend, she mentally corrected. She would have to see Marian again. She felt she had no choice.

Chapter Eleven

Bob sat on the top step of the porch, quietly humming a tune; his long legs were stretched down over the steps before him. Eloise drew the rocker next to the TV tray and settled down. The kids were out for the evening, Bobby over at his friend Sam's house watching a baseball game, and Caroline at work where she recently got a job waitressing at Frankfort Center's Roadside Diner.

"How'd your day go, babe?" Bob tipped up the sweating beer bottle and took a long pull.

Eloise watched the muscles in his throat working rhythmically, his protruding Adam's apple bobbing with each swallow. She loved to observe this very masculine part of him. Smiling to herself, she said, "It went well. Quiet. It was nice." She drank from her own bottle. The tangy brew was exceptionally pleasant-tasting tonight.

"Go anywhere? See anybody?"

She knew he worried that she was staying home too much, thinking too hard, not making enough of her vacation time. She'd heard his deep sighs when he wasn't aware she was listening. He would pause to look at their wedding photo on the end table in the living room, or watch her from the bed as she brushed out her hair before the dresser mirror each night. He didn't mention his concerns, but she'd heard his worried murmurs. "I chatted with some friends who dropped by." She would not lie, would *not*.

"Who's that?" he asked with interest. He pressed the cold bottle against his cheek.

"Oh, girlfriends who had the day off." So far no deceit.

He was still for a moment. "Colleague?"

"Yup." Just a small lie.

He took another swig and wiped his mouth with the back of his hand. Still staring outward, he said, "Thought you wanted to see some new faces, not talk shop. You're supposed to be taking a rest." He was angry with her.

"Oh, sweetie, we didn't talk shop," she said, rushing to placate him. "We talked about baking; we gossiped. You know, girl stuff. And we giggled." She refrained from mentioning that jealousy and war were also mentioned.

He rose and disappeared inside. She heard the refrigerator door open and close, then a brief hiss as he popped the cap off another beer. Returning, he sank again onto the porch. "I'm glad of that," he said, crossing his legs. "Too much work makes Jack a dull boy." She started to correct him, but he quickly added, a slight smile lifting the corners of his mouth, "Yes, yes, and Jill a dull girl."

"Do you think I'm dull?" she asked playfully.

He didn't answer as quickly as she thought he should, nor did he say anything like what she expected.

"Sometimes," he said.

His word cut her to shreds; heat burst forth from her cheeks. She'd set herself up for that one.

He continued, "But not often. We're all boring sometimes."

She glanced his way. He didn't seem to notice her dismay. He was so sure of himself, so calm, big, strong. For a moment, she wished she were a man in complete control of her world, where she could say anything she wanted without worrying a bit about hurting someone else. That's what Bob did—frequently to her, to the kids and, painfully embarrassingly, occasionally to her friends. She would later apologize, as had they from time to time for tactless or thoughtless comments made by their men.

"Nevertheless," she said honestly, "I've never found you boring."

He smiled. The light was fading. Soft shadows fell across his face, giving him a chiseled look. He could have been cast as a star in one of Cecil B. DeMille's Biblical epics.

"Oh, come on now." He reached for her hand across the table and caressed its tanned back. "There has to be some time or other when I've bored you to tears."

Her cheeks still burned as she continued to smart from his revelation. "No, never." She wanted to cry as she thought, I've bored him. No wonder he's always snapping. "Why don't you give me an example of when you find me boring? Maybe I can work on it."

He laughed quietly. "When you make me go to antique shops. When you remind me that lobsters make me sick."

"That's being a nag, not a bore," she pointed out.

"Well, then, maybe you're a nag, too." He roared at his own joke. The beer was mellowing him mightily tonight.

She withdrew her hand and rose. "Well, I'll try to do better, Bob. I'm sorry that I'm a bore *and* a nag. But," she said flippantly, "it's my duty as a good wife to be both. Read any of the romance novels, and you'll see that I'm right."

He chuckled. "While you're up, how about bringing me another beer?"

She did because it was easier to kowtow to him than not, to keep peace between them. As soon as she handed him the bottle, she pecked him on the cheek and went to bed, foregoing dinner. He said nothing to her as she left.

She woke and looked at the clock. Three A.M. Bob was snoring beside her. She never heard him come to bed. She was wide awake feeling energized enough to get up and clean the entire house. That wouldn't do. Everyone would rise like a cursed mummy and kill her for disturbing their sleep. Instead, she pushed herself to think only of good things. Perhaps then she could doze off.

She brought Marian to mind. She couldn't have a more positive thought than that. She envisioned her from the top of her small white cap to the tips of her toes. Actually, she had never seen Marian's toes, except when they'd all been children and she had been barefoot.

In her mind's eye she put a beautiful bonnet on Marian's head and saw her face in the shadows of the brim. How deep her eyes looked in the darkening light, a luscious brown, inviting Eloise to jump into a rich vat of chocolate, to coat herself with its creamy sweetness and swallow mouthfuls until she was sated. She envisioned the smiling lines of her tanned cheeks and saw her full lips, parted and revealing the crooked tooth that she had remembered all these years. Her thoughts moved to her tanned neck and deepening creases that weren't there when they were girls. She saw again the simple linen blouse, a fading brown, tucked into the even more faded long blue skirt brushing the ground. Still wide awake, she thought about the skirt. It was plain, gathered at the waist, making the hem fall in tiny ripples. The linen was wrinkled as only linen can be, giving the cloth a crushed-ice look. She stared at Marian's hips.

Eloise reached out and unfastened the skirt. It floated to the ground. Beneath it, Marian wore a cotton petticoat tied with narrow strings at the waist. She released the strings, letting the undergarment drop. She and Marian giggled. There was still long underwear to go.

"Here, let me help," Marian said, quickly slipping out of it.

She stood naked before Eloise from the waist down, the oak tree shading them from the hot afternoon sun. There was no breeze; the birds were still at this hour of the day.

With one arm, Eloise pulled Marian to her, then slid her free hand between Marian's thighs. She was warm there, burning Eloise's finger as she slipped it between Marian's lips. A burst of love besieged her and she felt herself climaxing, then a powerful sensation slammed into her side.

"Who is he?"

She awoke with a start. The jolt tore her hand from her crotch, and she scratched her skin in the process. My God, she thought, what am I *doing*?

"Who is who?" she snapped. He'd elbowed her! Her ribs hurt from his jab.

"You're playing with yourself! You gotta be thinking of somebody. Who the hell is he?" Bob was sitting up, looming over her. The light of tonight's full moon poured in through the window, and she could see the anger on his face, in his eyes.

"I was dreaming, for Christ's sake."

"Then, by God, I'm gonna make it real." He was on her at once.

She yielded instantly, not because she wanted him, but because it was quicker and easier for her and a hell of a lot safer than saying, "Not tonight, dear, I've got a headache."

In five minutes he was quiet again. Teary-eyed, she rolled over, careful to control any thoughts of Marian.

Chapter Twelve

It was Friday. She had come to her final inviolate day. After today, everyone would be home. Bob was working Saturday morning, but only for a short time. Caroline would work some of the time at the diner, and Bobby would probably hang out with his friends, but, realistically, she couldn't count on a full day's time without one of her family being at home.

She still lay awake, having been unable to sleep since four o'clock this morning. She heard Bob begin to stir. He rolled over and snuggled against her, resting his arm across her breasts. "Good morning, sweetheart."

She placed a hand on his arm. "Good morning, honey. How'd you sleep?"

She felt his smile against her shoulder. "Fine. You?"

She seethed and lied, "Great." Had he nothing to say about his outrageous behavior last night? Well, if she wanted any peace, she must forget about it, too.

He sighed deeply. "I still wonder who you were dreaming about last night."

"I have no idea that it was even anybody at all. Just some weird dream."

"You sure were into it." Now he sounded cross. "Well?"

"Well, what?" Good God, must she now monitor even her dreams? Struggling for control, she took a deep breath, allowing her muscles to relax.

"If it was just a dream, then why were you into it so much?"

"I'm getting up," she said, throwing aside the covers. She surrendered any thoughts of a peaceful beginning to this day as she angrily pulled on her robe and rammed her feet into her slippers. Belting the wrap with a yank, she snapped at him, "Why do you fart your brains out every night? Do you dream about eating big pots of beans?" She gave the belt another vicious tug, securing it painfully about her waist. "I never ask you what you dream about. Why do you ask me?"

He frowned and growled, "I wasn't complaining. I was just asking, for Christ's sake."

"You were complaining. You're jealous, aren't you? *Aren't* you? Jealous of a stupid dream." She didn't believe he had a jealous bone in his body. Maybe he didn't know it either until last night.

Having learned early in their marriage that she could seldom win an argument with him, she decided she'd better just stop her railing. Meanwhile, she'd give her hair a good brushing. That always seemed to make her feel better. She stood before the mirror running the brush through her hair with terse, angry strokes. Strands floated helter-skelter from her scalp, following the brush's movements. She looked like a porcupine.

"Just like a woman," he said.

"What? What is just like a woman?" She glared at his reflection in the mirror as he sat on the bed behind her. A superior look stared back at her.

"No woman," he said, "ever answers a man honestly."

The brush crashed against the dresser. "You think I'm lying to you? That everything I've ever said to you is a lie? That's what you think of me?" She grabbed the brush and again began to tear at her hair. "Sixteen years married and all this time you thought I was nothing but a liar. Boy, was I ever wrong about you."

"Now, honey, that's not what I meant." He sounded contrite. He came over to her and started to hug her from behind.

She twisted away from him. "That's exactly what you meant, Bob. And it's sick."

"You need to settle down," he said, pulling her away from the mirror and taking her in his arms. He began to laugh, to play with her. "You need to get your pretty head back into vacation mode. You've still got Saturday and Sunday left."

Oh, how she hated it when he patronized her. Her initial instinct was to push him away, but he'd hang on to her until she stopped struggling. He wouldn't make love to her now. There wasn't time.

She relaxed, letting him hold her and breathe into her hair. She deliberately sighed and rested her head against his chest and held him closely. Goddamn it, she was giving in to him *again*. But it was so much easier than arguing with him. She felt herself near tears. As she expected, he kissed her lightly, then headed for the shower.

She sat on the edge of the bed, feeling like a tattered rag doll with not enough stuffing left in her to have value. She listened to the water running and Bob's singing. That meant he felt good. Well, she felt awful. He was so loving, but he had these strange little quirks that were nearly intolerable. If she weren't careful, she'd be wallowing in self-pity and depression.

Her gaze fell upon the cedar chest. There was the answer to her melancholia. As soon as the house cleared, she'd dress and go visit her friends. Good Lord, was Eloise Hamilton—college graduate, wife, mother, nurse of the sick and elderly, owner of a home and car—really thinking like this? Wasn't this whole episode with the past just part of an out-of-control imagination to escape her present unhappy state of mind? Never mind, she told herself. If it feels good, then, by God, do it. Isn't that what all the bumper stickers said?

Thoughts of seeing Marian brightened her instantly. By the time Bob exited the shower, she was in a sparkling frame of mind. He asked again about her dream, but she fended off his questions, and he gave up trying to learn her dream-lover's identity. Privately, even she had a good laugh over who it was.

She waited for him to round the bend in the road before she tore upstairs to shower and dress. In twenty minutes, she was ready to venture forth. She realized she was manic. Too much happiness all at once. She stood before the screen door and collected her wits before leaving the kitchen. When she did, there was Marian and Agnes waiting over on the path for her.

What wonderful peace struck her, what joy. Nevertheless, trepidation stalked her as she joined them. She suspected her fears would last for a while—that is, at least until she knew for sure that in this era she wasn't going to die or become incarcerated and permanently planted here.

She greeted them with a big smile. "Good day to you both." They were dressed today as they were yesterday, same blouses, same skirts. No one had large wardrobes back then, she knew from her readings.

Neither she nor Marian made a move toward each other. There would be no hugs today. As long as she could see Marian, that would be enough. She was lying to herself. She wanted more than anything to hold this dear woman.

"I take it Mr. Bellwether is still away," Agnes said.

Eloise nodded. "I really don't know when he'll be back. He mentioned some big fort or other." Now, why had she thrown that in?

"I'd guess Niagara," Agnes answered knowledgeably. "There's always news coming back from that place. My, it's a good three weeks march away. I surely wouldn't want to go there."

Eloise tucked away the information for later scrutiny. "Well," she said, clapping her hands together. "I'd like to stroll about Tomstown today, ladies," she pronounced in a no-nonsense voice. She had to get into that town.

"I don't know about that," Agnes said. A wise-friend look crossed her face. "You know, loose tongues. If Enos finds out . . ."

"I can handle Enos," Eloise promised.

"And I don't see how he couldn't," Agnes continued, as if Eloise hadn't spoken.

"But he's my husband," Eloise argued. "I should be the one who decides. I can't possibly stay cooped up in that house day after day until he returns. For goodness' sake, is the whole town afraid of him?"

The sisters glanced at each other. "Sometimes," Agnes said. "His drinking and fighting at the tavern, you know . . ." Her face flushed deeply as her voice trailed off.

Of course Eloise didn't know it, and she was beginning to create a nasty picture of him. At any rate, she'd soon learn something about him.

They moved to other topics, Eloise accepting that the ladies weren't going to accompany her anywhere near the village.

Thickening clouds rolled in, blotting out the sun, the morning quickly cooling off.

"Rain coming," Marian announced.

"I wouldn't have guessed it an hour ago." Looking skyward Agnes added, "That'll take care of hanging out the clothes. Too bad." She smirked gleefully.

Eloise suppressed a smile as heavy, fat drops began to fall. She'd already known that rain was on the way. It had been on last evening's six o'clock newscast.

Marian leaped to her feet. "Time to go," she announced. Eloise and Agnes followed suit.

"I'll come back soon," Eloise said.

"Not if it's raining," Agnes declared. "My shoes get so slimy when they're wet."

"Same here," Marian agreed, greatly disappointing Eloise.

"All right, dear," Eloise said. "When we can." Rain was scheduled for at least the next two days. She could stand not seeing Marian until then. She could.

The sisters tied on their bonnets. Already they were hustling toward town as pelting rain coursed down in earnest.

For a moment, Eloise watched them hurrying along the path. Doubtful they had umbrellas, she thought. No, they had bonnets to protect them against the elements. If they caught a cold and got pneumonia, it could be fatal, as many illnesses were in their time.

At home, she slipped on her wedding band and earrings, then changed into dry clothing and hung the old-fashioned garb over the back of a kitchen chair to dry. Next, she headed straight for the desk and a fresh journal.

She concentrated on Enos Bellwether. He was probably not a significant person in the greater scheme of things. But he had lived here; that seemed a certainty. Lost in thought, she leaned her elbows on the desk and steepled her fingers, resting her chin. Her head suddenly popped up as she stared straight ahead but saw nothing. Perhaps the old family Bible was still here, stuffed away somewhere up in the attic! It might reveal something. She slapped herself in the forehead. Why hadn't she thought of it before?

A few minutes later, she sat in the attic, nude except for panties and sneakers, sweat streaming from her every pore. She had opened the windows at each end of the roof, but no breeze could fight the oppressive heat trapped in its apex even with the cooling rain.

Beneath a mountain of stuff—old toys the children had outgrown, red and green plastic bins filled with Christmas tree trimmings, hockey skates and sticks, cross-country and downhill skis, and ski poles, cartons of no-longer-fashionable clothing, crates of books and dozens of boxes of files from Bob's work and God alone knew what else that her family could not live without—lay an earlier generation of musty-smelling cartons, worn Oriental rugs, discarded brass lamps and outdated clothing sadly sagging on rusting wire hangers draped on worn clotheslines stretching from one nail to another across the rafters. Molding leather footwear, belts and even some ancient tack was heaped in one corner. All the years she had lived here, she had intended to go through this junk and get rid of it. Grandma and Grandpa were such pack rats that the task of cleaning the attic had seemed insurmountable.

Over the years she had come up here from time to time, aside from Christmas, poking her head through the door. After a rapid look around, immediately she descended the stairs, always saying the same old thing, "Another time when I have nothing else to do." And so she had left it undisturbed.

"Well, the time has come, hasn't it, Eloise?" she said into the blistering heat, thick dust and clinging cobwebs, many already netting her hair. At least she had been smart enough to bring along a small oscillating fan powered by a long extension cord plugged into the hallway below.

She felt claustrophobic and near panic, but too bad. There was a job to be done, and she was convinced she was in the right spot. The whole area was so chaotic that there was no good place to start, but she maneuvered her way around and over her family's heaping piles to her grandparents' belongings located in the farthest reaches of the room. Placing the fan on a box near her, she sat before it on a towel-draped box until the blowing heat gave her body an illusion of coolness. Mere movement started her gasping for breath and feeling faint. She guessed the temperature to be something over 100 degrees up here.

Where to start? Altogether, there were seven old trunks. In good condition, they would likely fetch a nice little bundle at any antique shop. She moved things from here to there, stacking and restacking until she could easily reach the old chests. They were packed tightly together, and it was a feat more of willpower than of strength to free one from the others before she could open it. The struggle left her limp and dazed and sweating. She couldn't go on unless she took a break. She'd die up here in this heat.

She descended to the hallway and went straight to the shower, turning on the cold water full blast. She let out a screech when the spray hit her, and she slid to the floor, letting the icy stream beat against her until she had regained her strength. Lifting her face, she opened her mouth; water poured downed her throat, cooling her internally as well as externally. Afterward, she lay soaking wet on the bed until she felt sure that she could again face the task before her. Why didn't she just wait for a cooler day? That'd be the smarter thing to do, but then she wouldn't be alone, and she wanted to be alone.

This time she brought with her a gallon of ice-cold Kool-Aid. She also draped wet towels around her neck and waist. Kneeling before the first trunk, she opened it and pawed her way past hand-woven soft woolen linens, tatted and crocheted doilies, linen and cotton pillowcases, sheets, table clothes and a couple of crocheted afghans. There were books dating back to the early 1800s, tin and wooden toys that today people would pay big bucks for, yellowed letters, old postcards, stereocards used in a stereopticon, that wonderful gadget. She remembered looking through one and seeing flat photos turn into realistic, three-dimensional scenes. She could have spent hours studying the trunk's contents, but she was searching for something else—a big book, thick and heavy, the old family Bible. She remembered that as a child Grandma had showed her the Bible one rainy day. Maybe Grandma herself had forgotten about the Book. She wasn't all that sharp in her mind those last few years, and Grandpa had died several years previously. The worse scenario would be that Grandma had already given the Bible to one of her four kids years ago. That would make it extremely difficult to access. The children were still scattered far and wide, especially far, with one child living as far west as California. No sane person would put such a precious document into the mail, and she sure couldn't just up and go get it one sunny afternoon.

She guzzled Kool-Aid and searched, guzzled and searched. Her nostrils were plugged with dust, and her eyes stung from her own salt. The towels she had wrapped around herself were long since discarded.

She still faced two unexplored trunks; discouragement lay heavy in her heart. So far their contents had all been similar: old clothing, pictures and linens, old Miss Goody books, a few Horatio Alger and Mark Twain first editions, some fine old china. Worthy things to be sure, but not what she needed.

She sat back on her haunches and dropped her head to her knees. "Damn," she yelled into the cavern of her thighs at the end of the sixth trunk. She rested a moment, then began digging again. Less cautious now in handling the delicate contents, and wanting only to get through this job and out of this hellhole, she carelessly clawed her way to the bottom of the final chest. Unexpectedly, she struck something hard and in her frustration, coupled with the heat, she screamed at it and shoved it aside. "Move it, you ancient piece of crap." But it didn't move, and she pushed even harder. The corner of a bed sheet flipped aside revealing a large, dark brown shape. She froze as she stared at what looked to be a leather-bound book. Slowly she pushed aside the sheet. With gentle, loving care she withdrew the item. She had found it. She had found the family Bible.

She took another moment to search for the diary that her grand-mother had kept up here, but it was nowhere to be found. No matter. No matter at all. She clearly remembered what she had read on those old pages so many years ago. Grandma's mother had writ-ten those words. She, too, had wondered about having missed her true love, her soul mate. She was plagued with the same questions that Eloise herself was now asking. Yes, she remembered it all so clearly now, and understood so perfectly what her great-grandmother was trying to deduce. But perhaps this Bible would reveal enough information about the family to answer both their questions. She didn't recall seeing any kind of record-keeping when she had first been shown the Bible. Likely, Grandma didn't trust her to touch such precious information—if it was there. She bowed her head over the Book, whispering, "Thank you, Grandma, for this Bible, and dear God, let a family tree be there."

Closing her eyes, she clutched the precious tome lovingly to her breast while rocking soothingly back and forth. She was so grateful, she nearly wept.

Using an old linen napkin, she wiped it free of every drop of perspiration. The volume was thick and weighty, and she handled it as though it were a newborn baby.

Sitting on the box with an old, cotton pillowcase extracted from the trunk laid across her knees, she rested the Bible on her lap, the fan still faithfully humming. The book was five inches thick, its covers worn and corners bent and frayed. Across the front in large, flaking gold print it read: THE HOLY BIBLE. She caressed the leather surface and then each letter.

Slowly, she opened the book to the first page. She went weak with relief. In penmanship as delicate as fine spider webs were written a series of entries. The work had been inscribed with a finely-nibbed pen and a black sustaining ink. Even tilting the book to catch the best light, she found the cursive difficult to read. Her eyes widened as she studied the first entry. This book couldn't be that old, could it? She peered more closely. Yes, she'd read it correctly. The date was April 17, 1754, the first entry made but without notation. Perhaps that was when the Bible was first purchased. The second entry was of Agnes's marriage to Thomas Whitehall of Albany, New York in 1757. Good Lord, she thought, Agnes was her grandmother's name. Marian's name followed although she had been born first. She had married Samuel Allen in 1754; no month was listed.

As the fan caressed her skin, its droning masking all other sounds, Eloise concentrated. Ignoring other entries, looking only for the Bellwether name, she guided her finger down the thin paper without touching the ink. There! Halfway down she found it. Enos Bellwether, son of John Bellwether, married to Prudence, daughter of John Jones and Hannah Finlay. Somehow Enos was a part of Marian's family, but no further entries were listed regarding Enos's own extended family.

She began at the top again. Squinting to make out the entries, she learned that Prudence and Joseph Jones were siblings. Joseph was the father of Marian and Agnes; John Bellwether was Enos's father.

That made her and Marian first cousins by marriage. She stopped reading through the rest of the family tree as a thrill passed through her body. She was pleased, very pleased.

Suddenly, a vice-like headache compressed her skull, attacking every square inch of its interior while she struggled to sort things out. The intense heat had finally gotten to her, she realized. The pain grew and her body began to tremble.

Half blind from the searing headache, she closed the Bible and wrapped it in the pillowcase. It took her three attempts to cover it carefully enough to protect it against her perspiring skin.

Descending the stairs was a nightmare, each step downward a dizzying experience until she reached the bottom. She stumbled into her room and lay the Bible on the bed. Her head splitting, she took another cold shower and sat slumped on the tile floor. Better that than collapsing, which she was certain she was going to do before this day was done.

She showered for a good half-hour, more from an inability to move rather than from cooling herself down. At last she dried off and dressed, then swallowed four aspirins. After stowing her antique clothing deep in the cedar chest, she put away the extension cord, ignoring the fan, and she collapsed face down on the bed. Before drifting off to sleep, she dragged the Bible, pillowcase and all, to her side, wrapped her arm around it and slept as though dead.

She awoke with a start. A car door had slammed. Damn! Bob was home. She looked at the clock. Five PM She bolted from the bed with the Bible in her arms. With frantic motions, she threw open the cedar chest and rammed the book all the way to the bottom.

"Honey, I'm home."

She relaxed. What was she getting so excited about? She was on vacation. She'd taken a nap. Yes, that would do. "I'm upstairs," she yelled.

Chapter Thirteen

"Want to take in a movie tonight?" Bob asked. "There's a comedy at the Strand."

"No, thanks," Eloise answered. They sat on the back porch watching the sun sink into the trees. Its glow backlighted them until leaves, branches and trunks became outlined in gold. Even at this distance it was possible to observe a slight breeze demanding that the forest shimmer mystically. Eloise was bewitched by its beauty.

It was Sunday, her final vacation day. The kids were hanging out on the deck; Bob was getting ready to barbeque hamburgers for them all. That left her no time at all to see Marian. But she could. She could. If she wore her costume with the nail tucked into the skirt pocket and sat just off the porch while they ate, she could see the town, its people, her friends. *Marian.*

"You don't want to go?" Bob seemed unduly surprised. "You've sat around this place for two weeks. Wouldn't you like to get out and go do something?" He stared at her, his hands restless as he spoke.

She didn't respond, didn't look to see his unsettled reaction to her refusal, she who never refused him anything. His suggestions were her commands, his wants hers to satisfy, his needs, hers to fulfill. "I'll be right back," she said and left him gazing after her.

She returned shortly and moved the rocker off the porch before reseating herself.

"What the fu—" Bob stopped mid-sentence, then said, "What in hell are you doing?"

"Relaxing," she told him. "Just relaxing."

"In *that*?"

"Yes, in this." She had changed from her shorts, sports bra and sandals to her 18th-century garb. She was still barefoot, as yet unable to solve that problem. She was at peace. Her "Enos" had returned from work, and he was content. No, he wasn't, but she was, and she thought herself as mad as a hatter for having revealed this part of herself to him.

Thus dressed, with the nail secure against her hip, she could easily see the village. Children romped, dogs yapped and followed close behind. Somebody called for someone else, but she couldn't make out the words from here. Marian appeared briefly in her yard. Even at this distance, Eloise could see how she was dressed. A small white bonnet was perched on top of braided graying hair curled around her head, her white apron protecting an ankle-length, brown linen dress. Eloise could only imagine her beautiful brown eyes and slightly tanned and gently aging face. Hoping to see her and then actually seeing her gave Eloise an electrifying jolt.

"What is *wrong* with you, Eloise?" There was anger in Bob's voice. She could hear it licking at her like a wayward flame. "*Look* at me!"

He demanded her attention, and she wanted more than anything to give it to him, but she was unable to tear her gaze away from Marian.

Marian soon strolled back into her house, and Eloise's heart settled down. Now she could look at Bob. "What is it, dear?"

"You're . . . you're having a fit or something," he exclaimed. "You look terrible!"

She felt herself coming back from someplace. Yes, from over there, from the direction of Tomstown. "I'm making believe that I'm living in the past," she said perfectly rationally. "You know, like my great-grandmother might have lived." A dreamlike sensation momentarily enveloped her.

"Well, damn it, I don't like it," he said. His voice shook. "For a minute there, you looked like you'd lost it."

Coming back to herself, she said, "Don't be silly. I'm just pretending, that's all."

"For God's sake, why?" He came over to her and stood beside her.

She shook her head. "I don't know. Just for fun, I guess."

"Well, go change." He wasn't asking her to change. He was telling her. "This is not fun!"

"No, I don't think I will," she said calmly. "I'm comfortable, and it's almost bedtime. I think I'll just stay dressed like this until then."

He reached down and tugged at her sleeve. "I think you should—"

"*Don't*," she screeched, jerking aside her arm. He withdrew his hand as though he'd been singed. "You might tear it, and then where would I be?" She stared as if accusing him of a sin worse than selling his soul.

"Naked, I guess," he answered. He was confused. She knew it, but she could do nothing for him except be kind to him.

"Please don't touch this cloth," she said. "It's old and it's frail. I'm sorry, honey, for yelling at you. Of course I'll go change. I'm being silly." She couldn't afford to have a thread of this garment damaged. How would she be able to replace it? How would she be able to see

Marian again, or to go scout out the town? She couldn't do it in the nude. Dear God, she couldn't lose these clothes!

She changed, then hid the nail deep in the chest before rejoining Bob on the porch.

After downing the rest of her beer she said enthusiastically, "Let's go see that comedy. I could use a good laugh." She did laugh then, a light, silly laugh, one that was totally false.

She awoke at midnight, hot and sweaty. The air was boiling in here tonight. Bob snored peacefully beside her, untroubled by the heat, his broad back resting lightly against her shoulder.

She rose and went downstairs. It was hot even out on the porch; she took along a glass of ice water and the sliver of nail she had stealthily removed from the chest. Wearing a thigh-length, light-weight T-shirt, she rocked and sipped, seeing only the town's outline beneath a half-concealed milky-looking waning moon and cloudy sky from where she had placed the chair a short distance from the porch. Not a star shown. Not a cricket chirped. Somewhere down the road a dog sporadically yipped; other than the melodic squeaking of the rocker, nothing seemed to move. Then, she ceased rocking as her mind cleared itself of all thoughts, as though preparing for a whole new idea. A wolf howled, the first time she'd heard one; but of course there would have been wolves back then. Plenty of them. She let the lobo's song sweep over her.

I could go over there right now, she thought. If I could get my clothes without waking Bob, I could go. The problem was that Bob seldom slept well if she wasn't there by his side. Would he sleep tonight? Lord, she prayed, make this be the one night he sleeps straight through. Suddenly, she was no longer sweating from heat but rather from anticipation and fear as the idea fermented.

She stole upstairs, waiting at the bedroom door to see if Bob moved. He didn't. She implored the Lord again. *Please, God, let Bob sleep. If you do, I'll give up cursing for an entire week.* She was wise enough to know her limitations.

Tiptoeing to the chest, she quietly withdrew the skirt and blouse. She heard Bob's weight shift. Heart pounding, she squatted down, lowered the lid, then froze. He settled down again, his breathing becoming slow and steady. She waited until she heard him begin to snore. When she was sure he was out, she bundled the clothing against her chest and crept from the room.

She didn't dress until she was out on the porch, making sure the nail was secure in her pocket. The dog still barked, but the sound didn't seem to be coming from the town. Barefoot, she slipped off the porch and made her way toward Tomstown. The bottoms of her feet were poked and pricked, each step forcing her to bite her lower lip to keep from crying out. She hadn't yet found some sort of decent footwear, and her feet were still tender from previous barefoot outings.

The path that Marian and Agnes took was well-worn, which made the going much easier. The dirt road into town was also smooth, likely due to the weight of wagon wheels and horses' hooves rendering it hard and flat during these unusually dry days. The road had to be a nightmare when it rained.

Standing at the edge of town, she could see only darkened forms of houses. Through opened windows she could hear people snoring. A baby cried, and a mother's soothing voice quieted it. Sounds carried great distances. She wondered if anyone ever forgot themselves and lustfully screamed in passion, or did they remain discreet and puritan? Likely, the latter. The question itself brought to mind the erotic dream she'd had of Marian and her. She felt herself flush to her toes. There she went again, with those foolish girlhood notions. Still, she gazed toward Marian's house a mere three doors down.

The temptation to go there was strong. She wouldn't knock on the door or make herself known in any way. It would be enough just to be closer to her. No, that was pure insanity. If she were discovered, there was no telling what might happen to her. She had come far enough for now—for tonight. She could come again another night—at any time she wished.

She was suddenly filled with exhilaration. Oh, my God, she had done it! She had transcended the present, had literally walked into the past. *I can come to see you, Marian,* she silently cried out. *I can hold you, tell you things that you cannot even begin to dream about. I could cure you of your ills and teach you better ways of living and—oh, Marian, if you only knew all that I know.* What a wonderful thing this was going to be for them both—and for the town, for their future.

She was overjoyed that she had come here and that she could return to her own home; she could travel between these two worlds at will. She was the most powerful woman she knew. Right now she felt she was the most powerful living being on earth!

She left the town's boundary and hurried home, stubbing her toes several times, followed by silent but sincere curses, her earlier vow to God forgotten. Stripping in the kitchen, she hid her clothes in the broom closet. Upstairs, she slid in beside Bob, who was still snoring. Checking the clock she saw that it was only three o'clock. In seconds she was asleep.

Chapter Fourteen

"What's up?" Bob stood at the foot of the stairs. "It's two o'clock in the morning." He had wrapped a towel around his waist before coming downstairs.

Barefoot, he padded over to where she sat bundled on the couch, feet curled beneath her, robe tucked around her, the dogs packed against her body. A book rested upon her lap with the table lamp casting soft light upon its pages. "I couldn't sleep," she said. He had invaded her space, her quiet time, her *secret*. Yet she smiled. "I thought I'd read for a bit."

His hair was rumpled, his eyes heavy-lidded with sleep, a needed shave in evidence upon his chiseled jaw. He looked at the floor as though studying it. A trifle of impatience in his tone, he said, "You've been doing this for a couple of nights now. You know I don't sleep well when you're not there."

How pathetically childlike he sounded. Her heart melted just a tad. She set aside the book and drew his body against her. She wrapped her arms around him, locking her hands around his buttocks, feeling his maleness against her cheek. He felt comforting—not sexually challenging, just pacifying, like a big overstuffed chair might feel if she were to cuddle up in it. "I know, honey, but it'll pass. Maybe it's that change-of-life thing again."

He ran his hands through her hair and over her ears, then stepped back and started for the staircase. "Good. I would certainly hope so."

His cold words cut her. "Why?"

He turned back, his hands outspread as though they could explain his comment for him. "Well, some of the older guys at work said their wives became absolute bitches when they started. I'd sure as hell hate to see that happen here." He smiled, infuriating her.

"Here?" she asked. "Here where? In my life? In yours? What?" Obviously, he had no idea what he had just said. She got up and angrily tossed the book onto the couch, the beagles scrambling to get out of her way. She ripped past him and headed upstairs.

"Oh, you know what I mean, honey." He was almost whining. "I just don't like unpleasantness, that's all."

Halfway to the top she stopped and looked down at him. "I know that," she said, keeping her voice low so as not to wake the kids. Boy, did she know it. "But, as big a shock as this may come to you and sad as it may be for you good old boys, women don't exactly have a choice in this matter."

"Well, they can damn well choose how they're going to behave," he said, now following her.

She stopped on the landing. "As though we were little girls to be scolded and sent to our rooms if we don't?"

He was two steps below her. Unless she moved, he couldn't pass her. She didn't move. "There's medicines and counselors for that stuff," he added.

Stuff! Jesus!

"Your point?"

117

"Actually, my point, Eloise," he said as if addressing a child, "is that you should come to bed—"

"I am," she pronounced.

He frowned. "—and not be wandering around every night, all night long."

"Oh, for Christ's sake!" She was in bed before he reached the door.

As he slipped between the sheets, he said, "You don't have to get so damned mad about it. All I'm asking is that you quit your nightly wanderings."

"And change my moods with meds and shrinks to suit your fragile male ego and its hallowed halls." She punched her pillow and slammed her head against it. "Men know so little about women that it's a wonder we ever got together to begin with."

"Well, hell," he muttered pounding his own pillow into a more comfortable mold. "You dames need us, and you know it."

She rolled toward him. "And what about the part where you need us . . . dames?"

He snorted a chuckle, and that was all.

"Well?" she snapped.

He didn't answer. He wouldn't. On those rare occasions when they bickered, this was usually how he halted their tiffs, by coldly ignoring her. She in turn would bend herself around to his way of thinking so that everything would be all right again. She'd bury her resentment, he'd become happy, she'd become almost happy, and their lives would carry on.

She looked at his broad back that she loved so much but was now so deliberately presented to her. Well, what was in a broad back? Hers was broad, too. Women had broad backs. Lots of times broader than any man's.

It was a warlike struggle to remain motionless beside him while angry heat seemed to radiate from his body. But she would keep the peace. If it killed her she would stay calm, and come morning, it would be as though nothing had occurred. But something had, and until Bob grew used to it, she would not—absolutely would not—stop getting up in the middle of the night to read. How else was she to be sure he would learn to sleep throughout the night without her beside him? After her first sortie to Marian's town, she realized she'd been damn lucky that Bob had slept throughout the night. She knew full well how restless he became without her there. He didn't know it, but he was in training for just that. Once she was sure he was of Olympic caliber, she'd be frequenting Marian's during this time.

The following night he again found her on the couch. They had a snarling argument, but this time she stayed put, and Bob returned to bed alone. A half-hour later she checked in on him. If he was awake and thrashing about, letting her know what discomfort she was putting him through, she would reconsider how else she might handle things, but giving up was out of the question. She found him spread out all over the bed and loudly snoring. When he slept three nights more in a row without stirring, she'd consider herself safe. She smiled smugly, then returned to the couch and read until four.

He didn't come to her again, and each night after a half-hour or so she crept upstairs to check on him, finding him asleep every time. He seemed to have given up winning this argument. If he had, it would be one of the few times she had ever gained the upper hand. She felt masterful and self-assured.

She ran her sleep test on him two additional nights to fully assure herself that he would sleep till morning. When, after the second night he did, she made her move. Knowing the kids never stirred at night, she felt secure that they wouldn't disturb her.

The following week, feeling safe enough to leave the house, she went to Tomstown several nights in a row, widely skirting the village proper. She wore her special clothing kept hidden these days in the broom closet. She became more accustomed to her route but hadn't yet dared to approach Marian's door. Still, she couldn't go on like this, just circling the town each night and doing little else.

Early Thursday morning, she returned home well past her usual time to leave, and even though Bob slept, she understood that each time she went to the village, her position was so precarious as to be idiotic. She knew so little of this era, she would not possibly be able to defend herself or explain her presence. Tonight, for some odd reason, the thought of how completely vulnerable she truly was increased her tension to near unbearable levels.

As she approached the back porch, the sound of male voices speaking in low, argumentative tones froze her in her tracks. Had Bob found her absent, come looking for her and, not finding her, in a panic sent for the police? He was so obviously concerned about her lately that her attempts to calm him did little good. And, too, if he was that worried, why wasn't the house lit up like Times Square, and men with flashlights walking the grounds? The kids too, would certainly be up, wide-eyed and scared. An overreacting parent could do that to a child, and Bob could certainly overreact to things.

Listening more closely, she placed the voices as coming from outdoors, around the east side of the house. Acidic bile welled up in her throat, but she was afraid to swallow. The voices continued, desperate but indistinguishable. She must get into the house undetected.

She managed to reach the screen door without arousing attention, mainly by holding her breath most of the way and taking the largest steps she could so that there were fewer of them. Her hand lay on the handle when the voices became clear.

A man spoke, his utterance gravelly and heavily burred. A not yet fully matured male voice, shaking and nervous, answered him.

"You *cannot* hide them here," the gravelly voice whispered harshly. "They'll be found before the week is out."

The more youthful man replied fretfully, "We have to. We'll be flogged if we don't." Eloise strained to listen further.

"Nonsense," came the burr. "Pass the word. Powder, too. It must be done Tuesday night. It's our only chance. Bellwether is purposely leaving Monday. His wife knows nothing. She'll think it's just boxes of supplies being stored here and later bound for Fort Niagara."

Bound for Niagara? That's where Enos was supposed to be now. That meant he was due to return home soon from wherever he really was at this time.

Eloise clutched the door handle and eased herself into the kitchen. She had overheard war talk. Those men were preparing themselves for something big. They were going to hide arms in the basement of this house. Tomorrow! She would go on living here, and nothing would happen in her world while her house was being used as an armory. Tomorrow she's check in the books she'd bought, one of which was the 1977 *World Almanac*, a reference book their house hadn't had, for what she was quite sure would be relevant dates. She'd learn exactly what was going on. At the moment, however, she could barely wait to crawl into bed smack-dab up against Bob's sometime angry broad back, which right now was definitely stronger than her own.

Once snuggled against him, she drank in his night odors, his manly sweat, listened to his snoring, which was exceptionally loud tonight. She was safe, glad that she was here. Those men, whoever they were and *whenever* they were, were more than welcome to go right on gabbing until their tongues fell out of their faces. She was staying put.

She sighed deeply, heartened that she was protected from this country's past dangers and destruction. She felt sheltered and secure—that is, until Marian's name popped into her head.

Then she became terrified all over again.

What would happen to Marian, now that the men were talking of war? What would happen to the women? Or the children? The children! She thought of her own. She certainly loved them enough to die for them, but, sorrowfully she had to admit in the deepest, darkest recesses of her innermost soul, she sometimes didn't like them very much. They could be bossy, like their father, and arrogant and rebellious, and had been since the days of their births.

They were their father's children, all right. She saw little of herself in them, which probably explained why she had so often felt somewhat left out of family events as they chatted their heads off. And now she worried about others' children long since dead and gone.

She rolled over, facing the wall. She felt so guilty. She could have helped her own kids more—gone to more basketball games with them, helped decorate the gym for school dances, visited the kids' classes more often on parent-visitation days.

Help me, she begged to Whomever listened to desperate cries in the night. *Help me to like my children more and to love my husband better. I'm a good mother and parent, and I feel like such a failure. Even more since I've somehow slipped into a time where I have no business being—but, God forgive me, I prefer to be.*

Prefer to be? Terror replaced a growing headache. It became a real thing with countless tentacles engulfing her thoughts, swallowing today and shoving her into yesterday. She tried to sit up but was weighted down by a cloak of living fear. She opened her mouth to scream but a tentacle slapped itself across her lips, clamping them shut so tightly that her teeth ached. She was smothering, fighting to get out of bed. Other tentacles picked her up and threw her to the floor. At last she could breath, could scream. Her voice shattered the air.

The sun was shining. She lay on the floor with Bob peering over the edge of the bed at her, a frown creasing his forehead and stark fear in his eyes. "You okay? You've fallen out of bed."

Dazed, she looked around. It had been a dream, a terrible dream. Already it was fading. She sat up. "It's so damned hot in here," she said groggily. She was sitting in a pool of her own perspiration.

"Night sweats," Bob said, his face relaxing, the fear fading from his eyes. He came around to her side to help her up. "I read up on menopause. You had night sweats."

Eloise brushed her hair from her eyes and crawled onto the bed. "Night sweats."

"Yeah," he said, sitting beside her. "Guess you had a bad dream to go with it."

She nodded, still in the grips of the dream but no longer remembering any of it. "I'll go shower." She felt his eyes on her as she entered the bathroom.

There would be no more. No more. Walks. At. Night. Welcomed icy water beat down on her as she made her decision. She would burn her clothing and throw the last piece of the old nail so far out into the field that she would never be able to find it again. But as she mentally played through this scenario, a fathomless ache engulfed her. She could not do it. Without those precious things she would never again see Marian.

The freezing water beat against her back while she leaned her forehead against the shower stall. She whispered, "I'm in love with her. I don't know how it's possible, but I am. She's a woman, and I love her like I've never loved another living soul." And Marian wasn't even that. Marian was dead!

A revelation struck her, and she laboriously thought it through. True it was that Marian herself was dead, but *souls* didn't die. She firmly believed that. Had she then been looking at souls and not at living people? Was she, in reality, not walking into the past but remaining within the present with her own newer history overlapping antiquity? Did events invariably repeat themselves, one piling on top of another forever and ever? Maybe history eventually arrived at its own conclusion, allowing time to begin again, completely duplicating itself with no changes, or perhaps with some improved changes, helping folks along until they finally got it right. It was possible. People didn't know everything.

She became uneasy and looked around the small fiberglass stall, furtively checking outside the shower curtain. Even now, someone two hundreds years hence could, at this moment, be standing near her, watching her shower, unable to communicate with her because he (or perhaps she, Eloise now admitted), couldn't find a way to step into this time warp.

She considered her own soul. If she were dead, would her spirit remain in the here and now, or could she join Marian? Did she have a choice? Was there a choice? And the dream, which she was now able only to recall how awful it had been—had it been a glimpse of hell? Was she being warned about what she would face at the end of her days for what she was doing—messing with time? Could she change her behavior, become a much better person than she presently was in order to avoid that abyss? Did it actually exist? Did Marian? Did she herself?

She cried. She would see Marian again. She had to. She felt crushed with sadness by what she saw as her only option. Not seeing Marian would be the same as already living in the Hades of her recent dream. She wouldn't bother Bob with all this strangeness, and she'd have to be very careful, keeping everything concealed. She would become a better wife to him at the same time that she saw Marian so that she wouldn't feel so guilty.

She shook her head while water and tears poured down her face. This was an unquestionable act, which she was compelled to fulfill, just as night brought morning and each season rolled into the next.

But *war*. She didn't want to be involved in the war. Bob had been to Korea. He'd been shot at, had shot at . . . He'd returned a damaged man, whereas before he had left she knew that he'd been a passionate, joyful boy. God, she didn't want a war; she didn't want to see it.

She turned off the water and toweled down trying to relax. Perhaps she was wrong. Possibly those men wanted only to store arms, not use them. Don't be a fool, she chided herself. Men did not store arms to not use them. They stored them for future use. *Future*. Again, tears sprang to her eyes. She knew too much.

Oh, Marian, she silently called out. *Can you hear me? Do you know how very deeply I love you and how fearful I've become for your life? Who are you? Why do you affect me like this? I'm so alone here, Marian. I wonder who it is that you talk to. I don't want to feel like this. I don't want to.*

Chapter Fifteen

It was the last Friday of June. With school out, the kids slept in. Only she and Bob sat at the breakfast table.

"You're not eating, Eloise."

She couldn't fool Bob. Still hidden behind the morning paper, he knew exactly what was going on. "I will," she said. Cereal and coffee sat untouched before her.

"When?" *Rattle rattle* went the paper.

"When I get ready," she snapped. "Good grief, Bob. Don't be so fussy."

"I worry about you."

"Don't."

"Yesterday, I made a doctor's appointment for you. It's at nine a.m. next Monday." He lowered the paper as he made his pronouncement.

She looked up from her bowl, an unappetizing spoonful of cereal and milk paused midway between the bowl and her mouth. "What for?"

"To check out this menopause thing," he said, folding the paper and carefully placing it beside his plate. "I want to know that you're okay."

She gave a little laugh, mixed with a touch of scorn. "I'm fine. Just doing my woman thing." Her smile broadened, and she shoved the cereal into her mouth, chewed and swallowed with gusto.

"You're different," he said bluntly.

A ripple of fear swam through her as she squelched a desire to scowl until her eyebrows became one. "Different?" The two of them sounded no better than a daytime soap opera.

He stared at her for a long time. She couldn't hold his gaze. "Is there someone else?" he asked tonelessly. "Someone at work? Or somebody you met during your vacation?"

She thought instantly of Marian standing before her for the first time, those dark, brown eyes gazing steadily into her own, graying brown hair dully shining in the sun's rays, her body garbed in ancient clothing. "No," she lied. "No one at all. I'm telling you, Bob, I truly believe that I'm premenopausal, and that's what you see."

"You still have your period every month." Well, wasn't he the observant one? "And you're still on the pill."

She nodded, embarrassed by his words yet unwilling to tell him to mind his own business.

"Then quit taking it."

She had, two years ago, still hoping for a child that was more like her than him or, for that matter, like either of their present offspring. But so far nothing had happened. "Of course," she agreed with open frankness. "If that's what you want."

"It's what you need."

She'd keep his appointment and then tell him what she already knew: Women get a little off kilter when going into menopause. That should settle him down for a while. Little did he know how many women took the pill because they were going into menopause. It helped regulate their bodies and kept them a lot more rational and calmer than their men ever knew.

This day's work dragged, and at its conclusion, Eloise was the first to leave her shift and the first out of the parking lot. She raced home, breaking most of the speed limits all the way. Rushing would put her at the house twenty minutes ahead of Bob, and give her plenty of time to study the east wall of the cellar for signs of an old doorway. Her grandparents had never spoken of one. Dirt completely surrounded the foundation.

She sailed into the driveway, turned off the motor and checked inside the house. Yes, the kids were out, Bobby probably with his buddies and Caroline at work now.

She immediately changed her clothes and went to where she had heard the men talking the night before last. There was nothing there except thick brush. She struggled through it until she reached the wall. Branches grabbed at her as she bent to scan the foundation built of quarried stone, one huge block carefully laid upon and overlapping the next, then mortared smartly into place. Old foundations built like this one were still in plentiful use today. Pulling back the brush as she went, she inspected the entire length of wall. She rounded the northern corner and continued her inspection. Halfway along the wall she found it—a section that did not match the pattern of the original builder's work. At some time or other, a gap had clearly been filled in with rocks neatly aligned one on top of the other and securely mortared in place. Satisfied and shaking with excitement, Eloise ran a finger down along one of the straight edges. Nodding, she whispered, "Yes, there was a door here at one time." She backed out of the brush and ran inside and down into the cellar.

Using the afternoon's golden light shining through two small windows, she walked over to where the door would once have been. A pile of junk was stacked against the wall: old boards that Bob wanted for antiquing the den (and over her dead body), a couple of galvanized tubs that had been there for as long as Eloise could remember, parts of an old bike half torn apart by Bobby, then left in a heap. She looked around; the whole cellar was a dump. That would have to change, and soon. Bob and the kids could clean it out over the weekend.

She moved the bike and tubs and pushed aside the lumber. It fell with a dusty thud, leaving enough of the wall clear for her to make a close inspection. That clinched it. Sure enough, this was where the door used to be.

She eyed the dirt floor, wondering what secrets might possibly lie beneath its surface. Okay, then, she would clean the cellar herself.

"All right," she said to the sealed entrance. "You exist. And this is where those men will come in tomorrow to store weapons."

She returned to the kitchen and made some iced tea. If Bob spotted her wandering around down in the cellar he'd ask questions. She never went downstairs. Another lie. She went there every time she hid or retrieved her journals.

It angered her that she was always so self-protective only to avoid discussions with him, and she'd been that way all of their married life. Why couldn't she just be looking for something? That wouldn't be like her, not to him it wouldn't, since she had vowed many times not to enter that spider-infested place.

She went to Tomstown again that night. How could she possibly stay away with Marian so near, knowing what an integral part of Eloise's life she had become?

By the light of the moon occasionally obscured by passing clouds, she boldly made her way toward the village one soundless step at a time. A couple of dogs barked as she neared the boundary, but after checking her out, they wandered off. They'd met her before.

Tonight she forced herself to go to Marian's. Relieved of imminent danger, she pushed open the gate and entered the tiny yard.

The house was a two-story slate-stone dwelling. There were two windows on the first level and two more directly above them on the second floor. A flag-stone path led from the gate to the house. Along the walk grew herbal plants, and along the front wall of the house were more herbs. Their aromas were strong and pleasant.

Placing her hand on the picket fence, she felt its unfinished roughness. A tiny splinter pierced her palm. She quickly withdrew her hand and sucked at the wound. Her mind churned with the question of whether or not to go through the gate and rap on the door. Frozen with indecision, she felt her heartbeat crashing against her ribs and blood pounding through her eardrums.

Withdrawing would be the intelligent thing to do. Her fear would dissipate with each retreating step, her heart would return to normal and her head would stop aching. Best of all she would be safe!

Enough beating around the bush, she scolded herself. Making her only choice, she knocked lightly. She could explain that she was fearful of being alone tonight what with Enos gone again and all. His frequent absences were beginning to wear on her. Her excuse was ready.

She would count to thirty. If the door didn't open by then she would leave.

Hinges creaked as the door yielded a crack. Even now a woman couldn't be too careful. Or was it "even back then"? Eloise wondered in a moment of insanity as the door slowly opened. She felt a gargantuan amount of relief at seeing Marian standing there.

"Oh, dear, oh, dear," Marian said fretfully. Dressed in a cream-colored, floor-length flannel nightgown, she gathered it around her and stepped aside. She touched her nightcap, straightening it, saying quietly but with obvious concern, "Come in, Eloise, come in." She did, then watched while Marian barred the door with a stout piece of wood placed across two brackets bolted on either side of the casing.

She was overwhelmed to actually see a Colonial house over two hundred years old in its original state. She drank in the dwelling's plain but comfortable details. Sleeping quarters were obviously upstairs by way of an opened, narrow staircase to the left under which sat a few dishes, utensils and cooking pots stacked on shelves; aromatic herbs hung neatly bundled from the shelves' edges. In the middle of the room was a plank table flanked by four unassuming chairs, not far from the large fireplace nestled in the right wall. Nearby, was a large pie-cupboard where, no doubt, nonperishable food was stored. Along the back wall, above a tin-lined drysink, was a window, a four-paned glass casing, that looked over the backyard. On the table, a chimney lantern gave off a warm, dim light. A large, circular rag rug graced the floor. The back door, made of wide oak planks, was also sealed with a crossbar. How absolutely simple and altogether adequate was this lifestyle, Eloise thought.

Marian took Eloise's hand. Without relinquishing her grip, she drew a chair from the table and seated her visitor, then placed a second chair to her right. Seating herself, she grasped Eloise's free hand and leaned toward her in a motherly way. "Oh, my dear, dear Eloise. Tell me what's happening? Why have you run away?"

Eloise's eyebrows rose. Smiling, she answered, "I haven't run away, Marian. I've just come to visit."

Marian straightened. "To visit? In the middle of the night?"

Had Eloise ever seen a sweeter-looking woman? She doubted it. She wanted to hold her. Now. Right now. She gripped Marian's hands tighter to prevent herself from leaping from her seat and swallowing Marian in her grasp. "Enos's gone off again. He won't be back for a few days, or maybe even weeks, for all I know. I couldn't sleep. I needed to see you."

Marian looked puzzled but considerably pleased. "About what, and in the middle of the night?" she asked, smiling widely. "My, my, my. I am so glad to see you."

"I . . . I just needed to, that's all." Eloise could come up with no rational reason or even a good lie. Perhaps there were none.

Marian's gaze held hers for several long seconds. She seemed to slip into Eloise's heart through her irises. Eloise tried to swallow, but her mouth was too dry. Without thinking she drew Marian's hands to her breast. Marian leaned forward awkwardly, then slipped to the floor, kneeling between Eloise's thighs, drawing her into her arms, tightly holding her. Eloise removed Marian's nightcap, then rested her cheek against the top of her head. Marian's hair smelled of lavender, and the silken, graying strands were soft and smooth.

They didn't speak but remained in position as though poised in a seasonal diorama. A clock ticked pleasantly somewhere to Eloise's left. The house creaked softly, as houses do. Marian's breathing was steady and comforting. Eloise felt the rise and fall of her hostess's chest against her, felt the pulse of her own heart beating against Marian. It occurred to Eloise that Marian might not be alone. She didn't relish the idea of someone walking in on them in this position. She asked, "Do you live alone?"

"No, Agnes lives here, too," came the muted reply. "But don't worry. She's upstairs, fast asleep." Eloise knew from reading through the Bible's family tree that both sisters had been married and widowed and that Marian had had a son, and Agnes, no children. With Agnes now alone, of course she would have been invited to live with her sister. "Agnes usually doesn't stir during the worst of thunderstorms," Marian added with a chuckle.

A tiny smile touched Eloise's lips. Then maybe Marian would stay where she was for a while longer. But it wasn't to be.

Releasing her, Marian said, "I need to get off my knees." She used Eloise's thighs to help raise herself and sat again. "Not as young as I used to be." Without undue shyness she again took Eloise's hands. Her cap rested in Eloise's lap.

"Linen or cotton?" Eloise asked, touching the headpiece.

"Cotton. I use linen for undergarments and dresses. Cotton's best for sleeping in. Softer, you know. And these hot nights . . . goodness."

"Of course."

It wasn't much of a conversation, but Eloise was satisfied, and it appeared that Marian was too. The important thing was that they were together. Without words Eloise felt it, and believed that Marian might, as well.

Even though fearful of breaking this suspended moment, she was deeply worried about Marian's safety. The Revolutionary War was occurring now. She asked, "Do you think the British will come this way?"

"I believe so." Eloise felt Marian's grip tighten and then tighten further.

"Do you have relatives who might fight?"

"No, no longer. But there are certainly friends." Marian paused. "War is a waste. A terrible, terrible waste." Her voice trembled. Lantern light highlighted tears in her eyes.

"I suppose Enos would go if it happened."

"I'm sure he would," Marian agreed. "All but the very oldest men and youngest boys will go, and all of them will think they're fighting for glory. I could tell them things that my ma told me that would smarten them right up, but they'd never listen."

"Men never do," Eloise affirmed, thinking of the millions of men and boys who were yet to go to war.

"Give them a couple of hundred years," Marian said. "Maybe they'll figure it out by then."

"I wouldn't count on it too much," Eloise answered.

She hadn't come here to discuss war with Marian, but what, she didn't know. But not war. Now, suddenly, she felt terrible.

Apparently sensing Eloise's mood change, Marian spread her knees creating a sagging tent between her thighs. She pulled Eloise toward her until it was Eloise's turn to kneel, to be held by this slight woman who seemed a tower of strength. Prudently, she kept her hands tucked against her stomach while Marian's arms rested lightly around Eloise's shoulders.

"Look, Eloise, whenever I need a good spiritual boost, I usually go work in my garden right out back of the house. The herbs give off wonderful smells, and I've planted vegetables too. Why don't we take a stroll out there? I'm sure you'll feel better if you do. I call it my 'healing place.'"

Eloise preferred to stay snuggled against Marian, but only because she didn't have to see anything, didn't have to look anywhere, had only to keep her eyes closed and absorb the sensation of protection while burrowed against Marian's bosom. Reluctantly she pulled away from the safe, miniature world of Marian's encircling arms and large comforting breasts. "It's pretty cloudy tonight."

"No, look, it's clearing off." Marian glanced through a front window. "The moon's up. It'll be lovely right now. Let's go."

Her enthusiasm was infectious, lifting Eloise's spirits.

Marian unbarred the rear door, letting them out. Eloise had seen this garden a number of times before, although not well, during her nightly forays.

The garden began within a few yards of the house. Beyond the garden was a large field in which Eloise had seen what she assumed to be Marian and Agnes's livestock—a milk cow, a couple of goats, and several chickens and ducks. They walked beneath an arched arbor bursting with climbing roses.

Marian said quietly, "These here are William Baffin roses," gesturing off-handedly toward the thorny plant. "Ma said William Baffin was an English explorer a couple hundred years ago. Somebody named this flower after him." They strolled along a winding flagstone path that separated the garden beds.

Keeping her voice equally low, Eloise said, "You seem to know quite a bit about horticulture."

"About what, dear?"

Eloise's stomach tightened. "About flowers and plants."

"Ma got me going. I can read, too. Her ma learned her, and she learned me." She chuckled to herself. "Now I've learned some of the girls in town to read."

"A frivolous pastime for women, no doubt," Eloise scoffed. Women doing anything intellectual at this time? A joke to be sure. She brushed against a bush and carefully drew her skirt in closer.

"The men think we're being silly and wasting our time, and I guess we are in a way." Marian paused to peer closely at a tomato plant. Offhandedly, she said, "Hm, got a few buds coming." Then she said in a bright whisper and giving Eloise's arm a conspiring squeeze, "It's fun to read."

"It's necessary," Eloise answered strongly.

Marian paused. "Do you really think so?"

"I do, indeed. Everybody should be able to read, and to add and subtract, too."

"Can you read?"

"I can."

In the silvery moonlight, Eloise could see Marian's pleased smile before she turned and continued on.

The garden was about a thousand square feet, tightly enclosed with a picket fence to deter unwanted guests. "I do have a time with rabbits and deer," Marian said in a low voice. "Not to mention woodchucks. I'm always working on replacing pickets the critters chew up. Look here, Eloise." Marian pointed to a semi-glowing, tall leafy plant. "This is lamb's ears. It's really soft in the spring when it's just a little plant. Feel." Eloise obeyed, already familiar with the plant that she considered a weed. Marian continued her narrative. "I've got all kinds of herbs and vegetables. And I've plenty of flowers. Here's some lilac. That's a butterfly bush. I like the smell they give off. Over there and there," she said, gesturing to the farthest corners of the garden, "I planted some 'old spice.' It's a really old herb. Dates back to sometime in the sixteen hundreds, Mama told me."

"That is old," Eloise agreed. She picked a number of different leaves and crushed them between her fingertips. The mints emitted delicious herbal odors of pineapple, honey-vanilla, chocolate, orange and others she couldn't identify. She herself once tried her hand at growing such flowery gardens and had fair success, but the aromas were never there. Nowadays, the plants had had the odors bred out of them for the sake of size and sturdiness unless one purchased heirloom varieties. Sadly, too few gardeners knew they existed.

She was shown the entire garden. Chives, rosemary, thyme, comfrey and a variety of sage plants grew there. "We'll dig up the potatoes in the fall and store them in cloth in the cold cellar over by the house there, but I'll wait for first frost before I bring in the squash," Marian said knowledgeably. "Much better flavor if you wait till then. Don't you think so?"

"Hmm," Eloise answered vaguely. She'd take Marian's word for it. "Do you have trouble with bugs this year?"

"Not much. I use a lot of horse and cow manure, and I toss all my garbage in here except for things that won't rot like chicken and beef bones. Right now, I've got a trowel lying around here somewhere that I lost last week. I'd sure like to find it. It's a good tool and the only one I've got."

"I could help you look for it," Eloise offered.

"Not now," Marian said. "It's too dark."

Eloise agreed. But she'd rent a metal detector and if the tool had any metal on it, which in all likelihood it did, she'd locate it and show Marian where it lay the next time she saw her. A sudden uneasiness came over her. "What time do you think it is, Marian?"

"About three I'd say."

Eloise knew she should return home soon. "Let's go back."

Inside again, Eloise said, "I'm feeling much better now. I think I'll run along home."

Marian nodded. "But let me give you a hug before you go." She stood on tiptoe and reached around Eloise's neck while burying her face in the hollow of Eloise's shoulder.

Marian smelled like a bedsheet freshly dried outdoors. Eloise drew her close, feeling her own heart hammering away. Marian drew back and looked up at Eloise. The lantern still burned, casting pinpoints of golden highlights in Marian's eyes. Her lips looked incredibly inviting. Eloise wanted to kiss her, wanted to engulf her.

They gazed at each other for a long time while Eloise battled a fiery desire to press her mouth against Marian's. Suddenly, Marian put her hand on the back of Eloise's head and drew her lips to her

135

own. Her kiss was gentle, warm, inviting. Eloise experienced the sensation of balmy water washing over her body.

Then they separated, their hands resting upon each other's arms. Marian led them through the front door. Hand-in-hand, they stood at the threshold of the house. There was enough moonlight so that Eloise could see the highlights in Marian's eyes. A ripple somewhat like a small electric current passed upward through her fingertips and into her arms, fading somewhere within the center of her chest. The jolt seemed to emanate from their clasped hands.

Marian's voice trembled as she whispered, "I feel strange . . . light-headed. Holy, almost. The ground," she said, looking down, "feels sacred. The soil beneath my feet . . ." Her voice trailed off into inaudible words.

Yes, that was how Eloise was feeling, as though together they had entered a paradisiacal retreat. A deep spiritual fulfillment touched her. "I must see you—often, Marian. I . . . must. I . . . can't explain it." Marian listened without moving. Eloise pushed on, not comprehending her own words. "I don't think I'll be a complete person if I don't. I'll be lost." She tossed back her head and looked at the stars, frustrated, pleading for understanding, not from Marian, but from something higher up, something more profound.

The electrical current continued upward, filling her as though she were but an empty sack. Her chest cavity was full, the sensation now extending down through her legs and feet, then traveling through her neck and throat. Her head felt as though it would burst at any moment. There was a second when she thought she might disintegrate into a pile of ash, but the sensation passed, and the fear that had been building steadily within her faded, leaving her with no memory of it. Left was the exigency of knowing that she must never, never be without access to Marian. To survive, she must see her.

She whispered, "I can't live without you, Marian." She should have felt silly speaking like this, as though she were a schoolgirl, but she didn't. She felt honest, and she felt pure. And if Marian wouldn't see her anymore, she would die just as surely as spring flowers faded away to nothingness at the end of each season.

"You'll see me, Eloise. As often as possible, for what good is life without you."

Eloise's heart soared. Marian stood on her tiptoes to raise herself eye-level with Eloise.

With her lips barely touching Eloise's, she said in a hushed voice, "I want you so close to me that you crush my bones. The church elders would curse and condemn me for saying this, but my soul belongs to you."

A flash of revelation burst upon Eloise. They *were* spiritually bound. Somehow their souls had found each other, over centuries of war and times of peace, industrial and cultural revolutions, whatever had occurred between Marian's time and her own, their spirits had longed for, sought and found each other. She said, "We can only be condemned if it is discovered how very much we love each other, Marian."

"They could run us out of town. Where, then, would we go?" Marian finally dropped her hands. Worry permeated her voice.

"There will never be anywhere they can send us or anything they can do to us that I can't handle," Eloise said. "I believe this with all my heart."

Marian walked a few steps toward the gate, her fingertips gently brushing at some tall herbs growing along the path. "You could never survive being thrown away into the woods, and to stay in Tomstown, we'd be shunned. Maybe even burned out. Your house and mine. And then where would we be? We're only women."

Eloise listened, her heart flogging her ribcage. Should she tell Marian who she was, where she really came from? No, not ever. Marian would never believe her. She might even think Eloise a witch, and not a soul mate at all.

"Please come here, Marian," Eloise said, beckoning her back to the safety of the house's shadows. Marian returned, and Eloise rested her hands on Marian's shoulders. She pressed her lips against

Marian's hair. "I'm very self-sufficient, Marian. We would never want for anything. We'll be very careful and not allow anyone to know about our love." She must lie. Yet again. She clenched her teeth, then said, "Enos wouldn't like it if you came to my house. He hates for anybody to come there except for his friends. But for right now, Marian, I can come to yours, and I can work in your garden with you. We'll grow wonderful crops. You and Agnes and I, and we'll put bushels of food by for wintertime. It'll be a good life."

"I wish I could live with you." Marian buried herself against Eloise's chest. "I wish that more than anything."

"You have your sister to keep you company."

"I want to lie with you."

Eloise closed her eyes. She hungered for the same thing—to hold Marian naked and warm against her skin, feel her curves, smell her smells, touch her nipples. Anguish gripped her, and she emitted a quiet moan.

In a kind of frantic desperation, they kissed again, their mouths opened, their tongues scraping teeth and tenderly sucking soft lips. They were one being in the deep inner recesses not of their bodies, but of their souls.

A cloud drifted across the moon, darkening the earth. Their lips parted as they tightly held each other. "I shall never, never leave you, Eloise. I swear to you whatever else happens, I will leave Tomstown and search the world over if we are ever parted." Marian's words were heated and forceful.

Eloise gripped Marian even tighter. "We will not be parted, Marian." Her body trembled as she firmly avowed, "Not ever."

But she didn't know how she was going to make this happen.

Chapter Sixteen

"Damn it, Eloise, it's pouring out here. You promised you'd come in. God! You're just like a little kid. I have to come out and get you." When the torrents had really started, Bob had come running out to her, one umbrella held over his head, and carrying another one for her. Reaching her he watched silently as she patiently and methodically swung the metal detector back and forth, scanning the ground where Marian's trowel possibly still lay some two hundred years earlier. If there was even a sliver of the tool left, the detector might find it. Bob stood restlessly beside her, his tall frame hunkered beneath the umbrella. Rain came pelting down. "Cripes, look at my pants," he complained heatedly. "I'm soaked up to my ass. Now, come on!" He thrust the second umbrella toward her.

He had been very clear about telling her how foolish she was for wasting good money renting a metal detector. It had taken her some research, but she'd finally found a place in Ilion to rent one.

"You're not gonna find anything in this field," he said with disdain. "It's been plowed darned near every year since before your grandparents lived here, and who knows how many years that's been? Anything good is probably buried six feet under by now."

She knew that but said anyway, "That's exactly why I want to check it out."

"I guess you're turning into an archeologist, huh?" He stood there, feet apart, chin tucked, lips tight. "You're a little crazy, you know that?" Then he took her in his arms and kissed her. "But I love you anyway, even though I wouldn't put it past you to stay here getting soaked to the bone just because you'd rather play than be warm and dry. Even the beagles know enough to stay inside on a day like this."

"Hold on," she said. "I'm almost done."

"Why in hell can't you do this some other time?" he asked. "A nice day would be a great idea!"

His sarcasm had no effect upon her. Marian needed her trowel, and if it were to be found, Eloise wanted to point out its location to her, tonight if possible.

A faint *beep beep beep* sounded from the detector. "I think I've found it, Bob."

"What? Found what? What're you looking for?"

She realized her mistake instantly. "Who knows?" she said happily. "You know how I love to pick up old junk."

"Hell, no, I don't know, Eloise. I don't know what it is you're looking for anymore. Come on, shut that damned thing off, and come back into the house before you catch a cold."

"In a minute," she said impatiently. She zeroed in with the detector until its blips were strong and steady. She turned it off and lay it on the ground beside her. With a trowel she had stuffed into her hip jeans pocket, she started to poke around into the ground. On the Fourth of July while the kids went off swimming, she and Bob had picnicked out here keeping their area as small as possible knowing that the farmer cutting and baling this field would not appreciate it being trampled down. The day had been hotter than Hades and the grass only half as high. They'd brought a blanket to sit on, the vegetation making the blanket feel springy and comfortable. Now at mid-July, the much taller grass dripped water onto her back and head while the sky above let loose with an even harder pelting, and she didn't give a damn about what the farmer thought about her digging up his haycrop. Tiny bits of hail were now added, stinging her as she knelt over the area. Ineffectively, Bob held the umbrella over her, the wind viciously knocking it back and forth.

Most of the grass slipped through her hands as she ripped it away. It was a dreadfully dry summer; the ground was hard to penetrate after the first rain-rich inch of soil. Still she worked, gently turning up dirt, folding it back as she dug.

Bob collapsed his umbrella and jammed it beneath his arm. He pulled at his wife, yelling at her. "Eloise, now!"

She yanked away from him. "No! I'll come in a minute." The reality was, she'd already been out here for a couple of hours finding a variety of junk: an old horseshoe, bits of nails, a silver spoon that may have some value—but no trowel. Perhaps Marian had already found it, and Eloise was wasting her money and time. But it hadn't been raining then, and Bob had left her alone.

She turned up a flat piece of badly rusting metal on the next hard yank of Timothy grass and leaned over to take a closer look.

"All right, then, *here!*" Bob tossed the extra umbrella down beside her nearly hitting her head with it. She ducked and looked up at him.

Frowning at him and frustrated at having been interrupted, she yelled, "What'd you do that for? I told you I'd be there in a minute."

"Whatever," he snapped back. He sloshed his way toward the house.

Eloise turned back to her work. Again, peering closely at what she had just unearthed, she studied its shape. Damn! Another old horseshoe. She gave up looking. Marian was just going to have to find her own trowel. It was just too cold and wet out here for her to look any further. She returned to the house, her knees shaking, so acute was her chill.

Feet propped up, Bob was in the living room relaxing in dry clothing. A real estate magazine lay in his lap. Heading upstairs for a hot shower, she said in a warm voice, "Thanks for bringing me the umbrella, honey."

He grunted a reply, not raising his eyes from the periodical.

She swallowed her unease. Of course he would still be angry, even though she had returned within a few minutes, just as she said she would.

In the shower, she let the hot water beat on her neck and back, loosening her tense muscles. She leaned against the side of the stall and rested while steam boiled up in thick clouds that got sucked through the ceiling fan vent.

Maybe she shouldn't go out tonight. Maybe she should ease up a bit on her excursions. She didn't think Bob knew she was taking nightly walks, but then again, maybe he did. Maybe he'd been watching her all along. What would he have seen? Her walking through the far side of the field gabbing to herself? Her standing alone in the grass with her arms around space, kissing air? If he followed her, did he hear her swear her love for someone else? *And a woman at that?* She hung her head not in shame or fear but in discouragement. She must deal with this in a realistic manner. She must bring the entire situation to some sort of conclusion. She had a life! A good life. No, she had two lives—and both were becoming so nerve-racking that she could think of little else.

"Oh, God," she pleaded helplessly and hopelessly. She did not have a clue as to what she should do. She only knew that what she had told Marian was true; she must see her again. Without her, she would never be a whole person. Not in this world.

Not in this world.

She raised her head. No, that could never be. Never. She had a world. Right here. A good world. A modern world, two healthy children, a husband who obviously loved and adored her in his own demanding way. She had a good job, money in the bank, access to hospitals and doctors, a car in her own time. The grocery stores were crammed with brightly colored packages of foods from all over the world; the meat, fish and poultry counters were packed, the vegetable bins piled high.

She had a life.

Slowly, she turned off the water, and the bathroom stilled. Only the drone of the fan continued. She flicked off its switch, too. Now there was only her sound, that of heavy breathing, the sound of fear. A thought grazed the surface of her mind, that irrational area of gray matter, the part most people used and of which few were aware. That was where her weighty creations were leading her now.

She toweled down until her skin glowed, dried her hair without combing it and creamed her body. She was a little chilly from the rain and pulled on a sweatshirt, loose denim pants and thick cotton socks. She wore her big, fuzzy slippers. Bob was probably right. She'd catch a cold if she didn't keep warm.

She'd go downstairs and make them both some hot herbal tea. She'd brew Bob a cup of raspberry, his favorite. Not say anything to him—just steep it and take it to him. She hadn't done that in a long time. It was one of the things she knew for certain that he loved about her—her willingness to do little things for him, like folding his socks in half as though they had just come new from the store instead of folding both top halves over and tucking one sock inside the other. At times, he was such an old fuddy-duddy. She wanted to say what an old woman he was, but the old women she knew didn't mind being fuddy-duddies, many of them believing they'd earned the right to be fussy after having been "givers" most or all of their lives, and she agreed with them.

She brought him a steaming cup, setting it on the table beside him. He lowered the magazine to his lap. At first he pursed his lips, then his face relaxed. "Thank you," he said and smiled. A truce. Well, that was what the tea was for.

143

"I'm sorry I angered you, honey," she said, crouching at his feet and placing her cup on the floor beside her. Immediately, she regretted her words. She was forever apologizing to him, only lately coming to realize just how often.

He reached down and patted her head. "You're forgiven," he said, stroking her hair.

Should she bark? Fetch his slippers? No, she had brought him a peace offering. She'd done her duty and obediently succumbed to his will. He was content. Therefore, she could relax.

In an unusual joint venture, both Caroline and Bobby had been planning a trip to Utica today, Sunday, with a few of their friends, but their driver couldn't make it. He'd been grounded for a week for denting his father's car when he backed into the garage. Caroline knew better than to ask for the car for such a long trip without her mother along. That left them the floor upon which they were sitting, and the TV, which they were avidly watching. A movie was playing. Eloise didn't know what it was about, but there was plenty of noise and lots of car chases going on.

Retrieving her tea, she settled on the couch, her slippered feet tucked beneath her. The beagles joined her, one on each side, crowding her. They flashed their doleful brown eyes at her and settled in. She pushed them away to give herself more room. They moved back in immediately. She gave up with a sigh and asked Bob, "What are you reading?"

"*Real Estate World*," he replied, momentarily glancing at her.

Gingerly, she sipped from her cup, savoring the steam rising into her face, the brew slightly searing her lips and tongue. Ah, the smell of mint. She loved the smell of mint. Marian had so many different types growing in her garden. She asked, "Honey, do you suppose if people of long ago knew a lot about medicine they would have lived longer?"

Caroline glanced back at her mother. Bobby was completely engrossed with the movie.

Bob looked up from his reading. "Are you serious?"

Wrong question. She was a nurse. She should already know the answer. "Yeah," she agreed. "What am I thinking? It goes without saying, doesn't it?"

He dropped his gaze to the magazine, saying, "Although there were all those old remedies that the pioneers used plus whatever else they learned from the Indians, I suppose."

Caroline gave her attention back to the TV.

Eloise was ecstatic. Bob had responded positively. Oh, why couldn't he be like this all the time? If he was, she wouldn't be looking into other worlds. If only he would support her no matter how outrageous she seemed to be at times. If he were like this she wouldn't even be thinking of other worlds.

What worlds?

Her brow furrowed as she tried to zero in on her chain of thoughts.

"What'er you thinking about," he asked.

"I was trying to remember something my grandmother told me. Something about mud and some kind of leaves for bee stings," she said. She hadn't been, but it was an acceptable response.

"When I was a Boy Scout," Bob said, closing the magazine but keeping his place with a finger, "I left the troop about the time the outdoor badge was coming up, so I don't know much medicine lore. Why, as a modern nurse, would you care about old medicines? It'd be like me wanting to sell sheds instead of houses." He picked up his magazine giving it a little shake and said, "Too much."

"You can say that again," she agreed, laughing as she considered looking into folklore medicine.

Chapter Seventeen

Eloise didn't get out that night or for several nights following. Caroline was presently flat on her back in bed, suffering from a summer flu bug. Not surprising. She was seventeen now, very attractive, popular, and constantly on the go. Eloise and Bob had both taken a heavy hand in teaching the kids all they could about how to protect themselves, how to keep safe in a world where few safe places were left. Yet, it was nearly impossible to convince a young adult of the value of appropriate diet and rest. Ignoring such basic and simple bodily needs, Caroline had overtired herself since school got out. Now here she was flat on her back.

A small nightlight near the bed glowed softly as Eloise gazed at her sweating daughter's feverish face. Several prescription bottles cluttered the nightstand. A humidifier emitted aromatic vapor into the air while an oscillating fan gently stirred the room's stuffy air.

After another loving glance at Caroline, she left, leaving the bedroom door opened a crack. She checked on Bobby in the next bedroom. Thank goodness, he seemed hale and hardy, still eating as though he never would again, full of energy and demands. He had fallen asleep with the bedside light on, a book opened and resting across his chest. She picked up the book and placed a marker in it before setting it aside, then flipped off the light. Bobby shifted slightly without waking. She brushed back his hair. He woke and rolled over. "Lemme alone, Mom."

She quickly withdrew her hand. All she had wanted to do was to gently touch him with love to assure herself that he was well. Well, she'd found out what she wanted to know.

Her face burned with rejection as she peeked in on Caroline one more time before going to bed. She was sure that if her daughter were feeling better, she too would shoo her away. According to numerous discussions with her colleagues around the luncheon table at work, aloofness was a condition of one's maturing children. The stand-offish, know-it-all, little grownups didn't want to be pampered by doting parents. It comforted Eloise to know that she wasn't the only parent in the world who had willful kids, but hers had been like this all their lives. She didn't get the impression from her coworkers that their kids had been so stubborn when they were little. They were also confident that their offspring would eventually shed their growing pains. Eloise seriously doubted that it would happen to her own.

Caroline stayed home for two weeks. During this time, Eloise took some time from work to stay with her.

In the interim, Bob nearly drove Eloise crazy with his hovering over Bobby, making sure he wasn't sick too and constantly popping in and out of Caroline's room, fetching her anything she wanted. When he got home from work each night, he'd bring her little gifts—stuffed toys, candy (the sight of which made Eloise's stomach turn), or a small bouquet of fresh, colorful flowers. Bobby, too, benefitted from his sister's illness. He received the same number of gifts but of a different nature—a new baseball, tickets to a concert in Utica that Bob took him to. He was acting the doting father all right, and the kids loved him for it. Yet the time Eloise spent with Caroline barely mattered compared to Dad's attention when he came home from work. It hurt, but Eloise said nothing. Daughters were hard to understand. So were sons, but somehow she expected them to be.

It had been so long since she had seen Marian. Her heart ached in so many ways—for Caroline, for Bobby's testiness—and because of her children's ever-present favoritism toward their father, who was spoiling them rotten. She didn't want that, of course. She only wanted equal love.

Sitting alone in the living room at two AM on this Friday morning, she'd completed any number of crossword puzzles, read several chapters of some mindless book, stared at the ceiling, the floor and all four walls until her eyes grew weary—and she thought about Marian.

She envisioned a brick building, a beautiful structure complete in every way except for the windows. There were no windows, and no matter how hard she tried she could not fill in that part of her fantasy. Those windows were a missing part of her. If Marian were here, she'd have no trouble completing her vision. But Marian would never be here. Eloise could only go there, but never for long. She wondered where Marian was buried. She seldom thought of Marian as being dead since she had only ever seen her alive, but if she did think of her as long gone, where would her grave lie? No, she couldn't think like that. Marian was alive, and probably wondering where Eloise was, why she hadn't shown up in so long. What would Eloise tell her? A lie? She would never be able to tell her the whole truth. She would have to become one of those close-mouthed types, the kind of person she had frequently longed to be because such personalities seemed to have strong characters. Eloise found that admirable. Quiet people were looked upon as having all the answers, as being somehow wise because they never spoke unless spoken to, and when they did, their words made sense. She supposed they were born thinkers. Well, that's what she'd become if she ever got to spend any length of time with Marian and certain questions were asked of her.

"Damn!" she whispered fiercely. Why was she just sitting here? Caroline was better now. Didn't she just go wandering all over the house today, eat three meals and demand that she be allowed to go to work tomorrow? Everybody was asleep, and it was a beautiful night.

From the top shelf of the broom closet, she pulled down an old grocery bag. Inside were her clothes and the bit of nail. In the darkness, she quickly changed and left the house.

Even with only the sliver of a moon tonight, there was enough light by which to make her way to Marian's. Now, if she could only wake her without rousing the rest of Tomstown.

Eloise was good now at moving quietly through the village. At Marian's door she was stopped dead in her tracks by three large dogs that had silently trotted up to her. She waited for them to bark and give her away. They didn't. She was familiar with many of the town's dogs from her earlier outings, and it took her a moment to recognize this batch. Lots of dogs in town had checked her out. Once they learned that she was a familiar, nighttime figure and not a wolf, large cat or bear, animals she knew lived in abundance at this time, she was of no danger to them. As the dogs greeted her with cautious sniffs, she carefully petted each one as they in turn inspected her feet and skirt before padding silently away. She let out a long controlled sigh.

She peeked in the windows but could see nothing. How was she to wake Marian? She knew the doors would be barred for the night, and she didn't dare knock as she had before. She had been lucky that no neighbors had heard her. She didn't trust that she would be so fortunate again.

With two upstairs windows, Eloise wondered if that meant two bedrooms as well. If so, which one might be Marian's? The idea of tossing pebbles at one of the windows was out. Not only might she select the wrong one, but her neighbors might hear the stones striking the glass as well. How was she to wake Marian without waking Agnes, and without frightening them both half to death?

The door opened on creaking iron hinges. Eloise leaped in her fright. She nearly collapsed with relief when she saw it was Marian standing at the door.

"I saw you coming. Come in." Eloise slipped inside as Marian barred the door. The lantern glowed on the table. "I'm such a light sleeper that anything will make me get up."

"Marian," Eloise whispered, taking her in her arms. Their lips met in fierce desperation.

Parting, Marian said, "Let's go to the garden. Sound sleeper that she is, there's no sense in taking chances waking Agnes."

Dulcet moonlight cast long silvery shadows over the garden and across the meadow.

"Come. Let's go to the field instead," she amended. The first cutting had already been harvested, and again the hay stood knee high; the wheat in the northern meadow still grew.

"Who helps you with your fieldwork?" Eloise asked as they circled the garden's picket fence and walked along the hayfield's edge.

"A real good neighbor. Fine man, him."

"If you don't mind my asking," Eloise said, feeling meddlesome just because she was asking, "how is he paid?" Doubtless this town saw much cash flow.

"He does all the work so he gets part of the hay he's put in his barn for us, and a quarter of our grain at harvest-time, and then Agnes and me will bake him four dried-apple pies midwinter. You saw the kitchen table and shelves. We already put up some vegetables and started pickling the cucumbers."

From her reading, Eloise knew that the entire town would industriously prepare for anything the coming winter might bring, even a raging blizzard. Bunches of drying herbs and beans would dangle from kitchen rafters. Dozens of quart-sized jars of fruits and vegetables, sealed against spoilage with wax and then with pewter lids would be stored in rootcellars, on shelves in the houses and beneath beds. In the corner of the house, Marian told her, burlap bags of corn seed would be stacked. A wooden box lined with a scrap of flannel would be purposefully planted next to the grain. Abiding within would live King George, the big, yellow mouser, keeper of the grain. No mouse would sample the seed while guarded by this alert and watchful feline.

Smoke from the community smokehouse would waft through the air while smoldering blocks of hickory slowly sealed in the flavors of venison, pork, beef and mutton suspended from rafters above, a task that would continue for weeks. Eloise had tasted smoked venison on a family trip to Wiliamsburg one year. Proper curing, she learned, meant stews later on and highly nourishing pemmican for winter hunting expeditions. The townsmen felled the trees the previous year, which allowed the thick trunks to season for the current year's smokehouse. Older boys were assigned the heavy responsibility of tending the coals, making sure that the embers burned steadily and evenly, for they were responsible for every family who chose to use the community smokehouse rather than using a smaller one of their own making.

Over the course of the years, she and Bob had taken the kids to several Colonial New England towns as well as to the Erie Canal Village in nearby Rome, New York, and the Fort at No. 4 in Charlestown, New Hampshire. In both Sturbridge Village, Massachusetts and Williamsburg, Virginia, they'd seen the authentic reenactments of the time.

The clouds moved back in, and the women felt free enough to wander over to the big oak where Eloise had once picnicked with her grandmother and later, with her children and, lately, alone.

On the far side of the field, they sat beneath the gigantic tree. They weren't that distant from town. They weren't even that far from her own house. As a little girl, this tree had seemed a million miles away, but as an adult, as she grew into her world, the distance to the tree had shrunk. Amazingly, it still grew healthy and strong. It was a wonder it had survived all the cutting around it. Yes, she thought, there is a God.

She thought that again as she sat and patted the ground beside her. Marian joined her, leaning against her. They lay back in each other's arms, their faces almost touching, swallowed up within the dark shadows of the great tree. Eloise knew every inch of Marian's face, every freckle, the crooked tooth she'd had all her life, the fine hair, the beginnings of a thickening waist.

"Oh, how I've missed you all these years," she said, brushing Marian's loose hairs from her cheek and forehead.

"I did too, Eloise. For a long time, I thought I'd die. The way your family just up and left. I never understood. People just don't go away like that. I thought the Indians got you."

"Some Indians might act like that, but very few, Marian. You'd be surprised at how kind and gentle they can be."

"I'll wait and see," Marian said skeptically, drawing Eloise's face to her own. "My husband was never as gentle as you are," she said.

"Was he a good man?"

"Yes, he was." Marian paused. "Yes, he was a very good man."

"And what happened?"

"Itchy feet for the Indian country. Got killed. I have a son too," she said, her eyes looking pained. "He took off when he was about fourteen. Said he was following his pa. I don't know . . ." Her voice trailed off and she rapidly blinked several times. "I do get a letter from him from time to time. Last one was two years ago. He's married, he says. He's got a son, too, he calls Chuck. Wished I could meet him." Again, her voice faded.

She didn't question Marian further about her family, but she was equally curious about why Agnes's husband wasn't around. "And Agnes's husband?"

"An accident. He was cutting down trees with some of the men. He didn't get out of the way in time."

At this time in history, old age was seldom seen, people's lives often taken either by illness or accident. Eloise had read in her almanac that in 1777, the average life expectancy was thirty-five. Marian and Agnes were well past that age. She had read in the family Bible's tree when both women were going to die. No, that wasn't correct. They were already dead. Butterflies churned in her stomach, and she dismissed this line of thinking.

"We make out all right," Marian said.

"And a wonderful job you do, too."

"I know it's a cool night, Eloise, and thank goodness for that, but could I put my head against your . . . skin . . . your . . . bosom?"

Now, for an altogether different reason, Eloise's butterflies increased. Her hands trembled as she sat up and untied the back of her blouse. She wouldn't think about the desire, the sweet longing to feel Marian's head upon her bared chest, the strangeness of it, the daring move she was making. She would be a modern woman and go with the flow and not be afraid or concerned or doubtful. She drew the blouse over her head and carefully spread it behind her. Lying down again, her breasts rested to each side of Marian's face. Marian took each one and drew them closer together before burying her face between the small mounds of flesh.

"They're so warm, so soft," Marian whispered, her lips tickling Eloise's skin and warming the spot against which she breathed.

Eloise could feel tiny scratches and pricks from Marian's rough and calloused palm as she guided a hardened nipple to her lips. The slight pain felt erotic, and Eloise heaved with pleasure. Marian drew first one breast to her mouth and then the other. Eloise found the sensations streaking from her breasts to her thighs maddening.

She turned and rolled over, positioning herself on top of Marian, then lifting Marian's dress, placed her hand between her thighs. Heat warmed her palm. Marian was like a little oven, and the pleasure of just resting there made Eloise more moist than she could ever recall. She removed her hand and eased her hips between Marian's thighs. Petticoat, dress—nothing mattered, nothing, nothing but moving rhythmically as Marian kissed first one of Eloise's nipples, then the other. Eloise anchored herself by gripping the dead grass on either side of Marian, pulling herself as close to her lover as she possibly could. She kissed Marian's hair, ears, eyes and mouth, all the while moving her hips.

Her orgasm built then blew apart into a million shards of moonlit slivers. She was made of stardust, downy feathers and ocean waves. When Eloise opened her eyes, tears were streaming down the sides of Marian's cheeks. She was panting and mumbling, "I love you, Eloise, I love you, my dear, dear Eloise. I love you."

Eloise replied, "Yes."

They lay unmoving, for there was no reason to move. They were one—one person, one soul, in the same place and time.

A twig snapped. Eloise jerked as though she had been shot. Marian wrapped her against her chest and put her hand against Eloise's head, pulling her face into the hollow of Marian's neck. "Don't breath," she whispered. "Don't move."

"Marian? Is that you?" Agnes must have awakened, discovered her sister nowhere about and come looking for her. "Marian? Where are you?"

Eloise dared not move a muscle. The heat from Marian's hand still pressing against her skull felt uncomfortably hot. Her own accelerating fear added to her rising temperature. Perspiration began to slide down her already sweating sides. The rivulets tickled maddingly. She wanted to pull away from Marian, claw at her ribs and breath cool night air. How quickly ecstasy could turn into a terrifying nightmare.

What was she *doing* in the arms of a woman, a dead one at that? Her heart skipped a beat. Agony filled her mind. How could it be otherwise? Marian was her *soul mate*, the person she had been born to find and to love and to hold as her own.

She felt the perspiration suddenly cease, heat recede from Marian's firm hand. Summer aromas wafted through the air—as did that of baking bread. She hadn't smelled that in a long time. Her tension lessened, and she sank comfortably against Marian as Marian pulled her closer still.

Eloise knew then that Agnes wouldn't discover her half-naked on top of her sister, smelling of sex and passion, their bodies covered with debris and their hair matted with crumpled leaves and twigs. No, getting caught wasn't the issue at all. It was something else altogether different.

New fears arose. How was she to accomplish her destiny? Their destiny, hers and Marian's together? She would have to leave all that she knew—her children, her job, her husband. What else, she wondered as she continued lying there as though dead, listening to Agnes softly calling in the night as she wandered back toward the house, "Marian, where are you?"

There would be health issues in the future. It was nearly impossible to rule out colon cancer. Seven members on her father's side had had it. Some lived; some died. Those who lived were only recent survivors. Medicine had advanced, to be sure, but none existed in this era. And Grandpa had had diabetes, and Mom, heart disease. Grandma had had a radical hysterectomy. Further, breast cancer was increasing. There was so little helpful medicine and knowledge here, and she was afraid. A geriatrics nurse saw a lot of patients slowly die for any number of reasons. Until the last moments for most, Eloise had seen stark fear in their eyes, silently pleading to any who would look into the depths of their souls, to save them from This Thing Called Death that was encroaching without mercy upon their bodies, and therefore upon their minds. Having comforted many of them, Eloise believed now that she had comforted no one. To die is to die, she thought, and all living organisms did it alone. If she belonged here, in this earlier time, if she lived here forever, she would die like that, slowly, fearfully, without comfort. A million Marians could be at her side, and it wouldn't matter.

She shifted slightly, renewed fright gripping her. She couldn't stay here. Not for another minute. Alone or not, she'd die a horrible, lingering death if she did. She started to rise, but Marian gripped her with arms that felt like bands of steel. Her hand pressed more firmly against Eloise's head. She blew into Eloise's ear, so softly that Eloise wasn't sure it was happening, but it was enough to settle her, to remind her that she was in Marian's arms.

If she kept still, she would be safe from Agnes, who must have gone inside, and from anything else that might cross her path. Her panic ebbed slightly.

Marian and Eloise remained motionless until they heard the back door close, the sounds carrying far across the field. Marian released Eloise, and Eloise rolled to her side exhaling a deep breath she hadn't even realized she'd been holding.

"Oh, my God," she whispered. "I've never been so scared in my life." She began to shiver, from the cool night air or evaporating sweat she wasn't sure.

"Why?" Marian asked, shifting to Eloise's side while keeping her arm draped across Eloise's chest. Her hand cupped Eloise's breast. "Agnes would be shocked, but she wouldn't shoot us."

Eloise sat up and drew on her blouse, feeling much more protected dressed than nude. She breathed deeply, saying, "You know your sister better than I do, Marian. I just hope you're right." She trembled so, she could barely retie the strings at the back of her blouse.

"And if I'm not? So what?" Marian straightened her clothing. On their feet again, Marian put her arms around Eloise's neck. Feeling not at all comforted, she only wanted to be gone from here. She needed space; a universe's worth would do nicely. She was running between pure fear and pure elation and desperately needed time to straight-line her emotions.

"Come on," Marian invited, "let's go over to the creek."

"No, I must go, Marian. I've been away too long." She needed to leave Marian and return to her normal life. Right now, this one was too frightening, more so than believing she was with her soul mate.

"You've been gone not much over an hour yet," Marian pleaded. "I've been watching the moon and stars through the clouds."

"You're quite clever at telling time by the stars," Eloise said, holding Marian's hands and looking into her eyes. "You're clever at so many things." As wonderful and near-miraculous as modern progress was, it had lost so much to time. "An hour is long enough. I must go."

"When will you be back?"

"Soon," Eloise answered, deliberately remaining vague. She had much to sort out and to consider.

Marian walked her to the front gate. Eloise wouldn't let her go farther. No sense in two of them getting caught wandering around in the dark. It was a wonder that the dogs hadn't set off an alarm.

As she entered her own back door, she shrieked. Bob stood there, a large shadow in the dark. "Where'd you go?" he asked. "And in those goddamn old clothes again."

She flicked on the light and squinted against its brightness. He was naked, his body ready for her.

The skin on her scalp crawled as she looked at his sneakered feet. Had he followed her, watched her making love? He wouldn't have been able to see anything other than his wife screwing the hell out of the ground and talking to herself. "I took a walk," she answered lamely.

"You sure as hell did." He was furious, his face taut, his neck muscles stretched. "Why didn't you tell me you were horny?"

Her face remained impassive, but inside she recoiled. She hated that word. "Excuse me?" she said flippantly. She began to make a pot of coffee, aware of the debris in her hair and the mess her old clothes were in.

His eyes followed her, heavy-lidded, hot, angry. "I saw you fucking yourself over by the tree. I thought about screwing you right then and there, but the show was too good. And who the hell is Marian?"

Chapter Eighteen

It was over. Thank God it was over and Bob had turned on his side and slept. He had hurt her; for the first time in their sexual lives, he had hurt her. How could she possibly feel such a sense of disjointedness? How could she feel such love of a woman and that of a man, too? She knew she loved Bob. Knew it as well as she knew her own name.

But he isn't your soul mate. Marian is.

The words jumped out at her. No, it can't be, she silently cried out. It's impossible! Women do not love women like that! Not like *that!*

Yes, they do.

She nodded against her pillow, minutely so as not to disturb Bob. Yes, they do, she agreed with whatever internal voice argued with her. She recalled her college days. Women, *lesbians*—she had barely been able to utter the word—were making themselves known on campus at the University of Buffalo. They had some sort of club downstairs in the student union. They wore jeans and short hair and were generally hard-looking, but some were very beautiful. It was the beautiful ones who confused Eloise. How could a woman look that gorgeous and still hang out with lesbians? Beautiful women married. Always!

She glanced at the bedside clock. The red digital numbers told her it was only three-thirty A.M. She rolled onto her back and lay staring at the ceiling. Maybe she was going stark raving mad. Maybe none of this was happening.

For the next two weeks after work, Eloise haunted the library, scouring delicate, antique books kept securely under lock and key and loaned only upon direct request. Her excuse to her family for her lateness each evening was that it was much wiser spending an hour or so in the air-conditioned library than coming directly home to cook dinner where, as cool as old farmhouses usually were just by the nature of their structure, this summer was too hot even for their big airy house. They muttered their unhappiness that they didn't have access to the same luxury, but she often pacified them by stopping at the store for a quart of ice cream, an extra treat after dinner.

At the library, she read all she could about Herkimer County, its beginnings, its growth and its place in present day. She finally learned from one ancient, that Tomstown, once located near her road, but now completely obscured by time and elements, had eventually been deserted. One by one its residents had moved to larger villages. She thought it likely that that was how so many Bellwethers had ended up in Utica.

No longer feeling secure leaving her journals at home, she rented a safe-deposit box in the Ilion bank near where she worked.

During the end of the second week, she rented a motel room east of Herkimer, for the following weekend. Not much chance of Bob's finding her there. Most of his business took place in Ilion, to the west of Herkimer. She told Bob she'd like to spend the weekend in Utica with her best friend, Janie Siva, from college days, and who now taught at Utica College. They often spoke on the phone and occasionally visited each other. Bob liked Janie for her high spirits and frank and honest opinions.

Surprisingly, he encouraged his wife. "You should go visit," he agreed, taking her in his arms. "You need a change of scenery. We'll be fine here, honey, don't worry."

She felt his smile against her cheek. He was being so cooperative and sweet that she nearly changed her mind. She planned to call him from the motel room, letting him know that she'd arrived safely at Janie's, thus assuring him that he wouldn't need to call there except for an emergency, and she seriously doubted that one would arise.

Leaving directly from work that Friday evening, she retrieved her cache of journals from the bank's vault, stuffing the literature into her tote bag before stopping at a grocery store along the way, one nowhere near where she might be recognized, to stock up on anything that wouldn't spoil over a weekend. She loaded her cart with pickles, potato chips, dips, canned sodas, instant coffee, bread, instant soups, peanut butter, grape jelly and peach jam.

At the Roadside Motel she settled in, first phoning Bob, then leaving the receiver off the hook just in case it might even mistakenly ring. She turned the TV screen toward the wall. On a small, circular table, she placed her tote bag and, with near reverence, withdrew its contents.

Methodically, slowly, she caressed each journal, book and pamphlet she had picked up here and there and gathered over the last few months. She had her almanac with her and three volumes of the *Britannica* she'd also brought—one giving information regarding General Herkimer, another on Colonial life and the last regarding bee-raising. She had wanted to bring along several more volumes, but it would be too obvious that part of the set was clearly missing. A book or two wasn't out of the ordinary to be in one of the kids' room or lying around in the living room somewhere, but more than that was out of the question.

She organized the materials, sorting them into time periods, clothing styles, medicines and herbs, food, livelihoods, domestic animals, housing, politics and miscellaneous. Feeling euphoric and confident, she sat in a thickly padded plastic chair and began reading. Before she went home Sunday evening, she would know most if not all of what was on these pages. She would understand differences and likenesses of that time and of this time. She would put them together and make them work for her—for the "then" and for the "now".

By Sunday evening she figured she knew more about Herkimer County and its great history than did most of its residents. She was quite sure she knew the time to the day that General Herkimer and his troops would be marching through Tomstown on their way to Oriskany searching for the hidden Tory arms in her house. It was documented here and there throughout her readings. She sat musing, finding all this exceedingly interesting.

Chapter Nineteen

Eloise drove home with a head full of ideas. She was going to change her life, not that that hadn't already happened in smart style, but she was going to live as Marian lived; she'd grow her own crops, have Bob hire somebody to put in a pump well so that she would have to pump and haul water as Marian did. She would learn to be a hell of a seamstress and sew all her own clothing and maybe even Bob's and the kids'. No, not the kids'. They'd balk all the way. Bob's and her clothes, then. She'd sew by hand. Maybe she could learn to use a loom and learn to spin and weave. She could take a class at the historical society. She wouldn't have time to work anymore. Bob would have to carry the ball there, but she could help by canning food processed outdoors over a cauldron heated with wood. She could sell vegetables and eggs too, once she bought some laying hens. She could also sell honey and make candles. That was easy enough. If she raised bees, she could make the candles from rolled beeswax. Her head rang with plans; her heart raced with excitement. She could hardly wait to get home and tell Bob. She would also be able to better assist Marian during the war. This year, she reasoned, because the growing season was almost over, she'd have to buy her vegetables and fruits to can. She'd have to buy wax to make candles, but next year . . . Well, next year she'd be right on top of everything.

Wanting to further think through the best way to present things to him, she waited until Monday evening. The more she considered her aims, the better she liked them. After all, Bob did like some old things—old architecture, an occasional piece of antique furniture, homemade baked goods. She was sure he would actually enjoy his totally domesticated wife and might even prefer her this way.

That evening after dinner, she called the family together in the living room. "Bobby, Caroline, sit on the sofa," she began. "Bob, take a seat in your chair." She breathed deeply, scared, excited and anxious to tell them. She remained on her feet, standing before them much as a teacher might stand before a class. Taking another deep breath while her brood stared at her with concern and interest at this, the first family meeting in their lives, she began by telling the truth of where she had been this weekend and apologizing profusely for her deceit. "I needed to be alone," she said quickly, seeing the disbelieving look in Bob's eyes. "I was afraid that you would pooh-pooh my idea."

"You lied." His cheek muscles twitched.

"Well, yes," she said slowly, "and I am so sorry about that, but I really needed to be alone and away from here, where I could think uninterrupted, but here's why I did." He opened his mouth to speak, his brows furrowing, his face set in anger. She jumped in, saying, "Please, Bob, just listen to me, please." And then she laid out her entire proposal before him and her children.

"You are losing it, Eloise. *Losing* it!" Bob glared at her from his Lazy Boy. His feet straddled the raised ottoman as he sat leaning over it. "I want you to get rid of that junk!" He made a sweeping gesture toward the books, magazines and pamphlets covering the coffee table where she had displayed them, having taken the journals to the safe-deposit box on her lunch break.

She had wanted his full attention while she explained from beginning to end, and without interruption, her new plans for their life. This was the twentieth century, and she *was* a modern woman. Now, from across the room he was belittling her. The kids were clearly uncomfortable. Bobby was sprawled on the couch, his legs straight out and his eyes clouded; Caroline sat primly, looking critical if not downright hostile.

"This is bull!" Bob shouted at her, and everyone jumped. He leaped over the footrest; in two strides he was across the room shoving her materials to the floor. "This is bull," he yelled again as he began kicking the books all over the floor. "Get rid of this shit." He whirled on her. "Get rid of that old clothing in the kitchen closet, too. We're selling this goddamn place!" His face was dangerously red.

She feared he would have a stroke or heart attack, and never before had she feared for herself *and* for the children. They had never seen their father so completely enraged. Both of them rose to escape.

"*Sit down!*" Bob bellowed. They did, their eyes wide and uncomprehending. "This whole household is out of control!" Bobby started to say something, but Bob cut him off. "Shut up, Bobby! I'm telling you people right now that I'm sick of all this nonsense that's going on."

"What, Dad?" Caroline meekly asked.

"Your mother, that's what. Your mother. She wanders around at night in old clothes, rags, in the dead of night . . . You better be telling Dr. Strictland about this." She hadn't told him that she had stopped therapy some time ago. He'd really blow up if he knew that! "Or go back to church. You used to go to the Methodist Church. Why not go again?"

Because the rules were just too many for her to obey. The kids occasionally took the car and attended, but Bob, never. He was a fine one to be telling her to go.

Oh, please, Eloise silently begged him, don't tell the kids all of it. She was thinking of the time when Bob thought he saw her masturbating.

"Damn!" He stood, his fists balled against his hips, like an enraged Superman.

"Mom?" Caroline said.

Bob was panting as though he'd been running uphill for hours. His breath whistled though his nose, and beads of sweat protruded from his forehead.

Eloise looked at her wide-eyed daughter. "Yes, honey?" She struggled to stay calm.

Her eyes wide with fright, Caroline hesitated before saying, "Maybe Dad's right . . ."

"He's right," Bobby chirped in.

Caroline flashed him an irritated look, then said to Eloise, "Maybe you could find another hobby. You know, like, maybe . . ."

"You're stuttering, Caroline. Speak up."

"Well, like . . ." It was plain that she was struggling to put forth her thoughts in a tactful way.

She hadn't practiced tact in all her life. I have failed her, Eloise thought. And the rest of them.

Caroline continued, pausing, carefully choosing her words. "There's stuff that goes on at church, like, you know, like spaghetti dinners and stuff like that, and the hospital could use volunteers."

Eloise stood amid the jumble of papers and books. "Oh, what do you know, Caroline, about volunteering? And must I remind you that I work in a hospital? Why would I want to volunteer there, too? Use your head." She was so angry, she couldn't be kind.

"She's only trying to be helpful, Mom." Bobby sat upright on the sofa.

"I see." She looked at each one in turn, then at Bob. "And you, you want me to stop this . . . this hobby, is that right? All of you want me to stop, is that right?"

"Absolutely, and now!" Bob yelled, answering for them all.

"No need to shout." She bent over and began to retrieve her precious materials. The kids jumped up to help.

"No," she said, holding up a hand as if to stop traffic. "I can manage."

"And burn it!" Bob shouted.

She paused as she clutched another pamphlet. "Burn it?" she asked in disbelief.

"Today, now."

"Later, after I've rested."

"Now!"

"All right, now." She put the papers in a wastebasket and took them outdoors. She tossed the papers into the burn barrel, then lit them. They torched quickly, turning to white ash that rose and floated above her and out toward the field where Marian lived.

"Here!" Bob was hustling toward her with her precious antique clothing in his arms. "Get rid of these rags too." Obviously he had known where she kept them hidden.

She stepped aside while he threw them in. She watched. They were soon gone. No matter. She had one thing that he could not destroy, at least not so far, and that was her mind.

And, of course, all her journals were still safe, not that they could take her where she wanted to go, but they were protected.

And in the far corner of that old broom closet was just the tiniest bit of antiquated nail.

Chapter Twenty

She'd left work early today, angering her supervisor, but it no longer mattered what her supervisor thought. Standing in the kitchen, she first took a look at the calendar hanging on the wall—August 4, 1977—and then an even longer and more leisurely look at every room in the old house, starting upstairs in the bedroom, where for years she had lain safe in Bob's strong arms. There at the dresser mirror, she had brushed her hair and felt Bob's arms slip around her waist. She could smell his odor, hers, theirs. They had made love only last night. She had thrown herself into their passion, assuring herself that she gave to him all that she could and took from him all that he was able to give.

The kids were out right now, Caroline at work, Bobby off with his pals, so she took the time to sit resting on each of their beds, running her hands across the summer blankets under which they slept each night. She picked up their pillows and inhaled their scents,

Bobby's becoming very masculine, Caroline's traced with perfume, which smelled suspiciously like her own. Eloise smiled. How many times had she told Caroline to leave her perfumes alone? Downstairs she wandered throughout the house touching this and that, picking up knickknacks, remembering their little histories, their little memories.

This house had been her life since childhood. It was rich with the family's history—and her story. If her children were insightful enough, one or both of them would want to learn about it. Perhaps one day, they would care. Meanwhile she had written a detailed account of it all, from her childhood days while visiting here up through yesterday. All the information was in her safe-deposit box, plus her journals and a few ashes from her incinerated clothing that she had managed to salvage from the burn barrel.

She felt her resolve stiffen as she concentrated on what had led her to this point: lack of appreciation or affection and love from her family and the love of another family that awaited her. All she had to do was take the final step to get it all right this time.

She checked her watch, then removed it along with her wedding band and earrings, setting them ceremoniously in the middle of the kitchen table. She sat at the small rolltop desk in the living room at which she had written so many notes. In one of the side drawers was kept her safe-deposit box key. She unlocked the drawer and removed it, then placed it beside her other jewelry on the kitchen table.

It was nearly time now. General Herkimer would be here at any moment. She had finally figured out why this house had been rebuilt. Herkimer's army had once leveled a cannon at it and blown it to smithereens on this date. He had to have known that Bellwether was storing British arms here. How he learned this fact she didn't know. The history books hadn't been clear on that point. Likely too, some previous history buff had learned the ill-fated house's history and was perhaps a friend of England, or just liked the location and architecture of the previous structure and had therefore rebuilt the house. Thus, if she could put herself in Herkimer's time and not in her own when the building was destroyed, it would still be standing according to Bob. Only she would have disappeared forever. He would believe that she had finally lost all sanity and run away never to be found again. Just she and the house as she knew it right now would be gone.

She was being selfish to the point of cruelty, but she couldn't stop herself. She mourned for what her family would go through, what people would say, what her children would suffer. She was experiencing a crisis of the soul and saw only suicide in her future if she stayed. That would be worse for them, bringing more shame to them that they hadn't seen things better, hadn't heard her at all, hadn't listened.

Oh, my children, my children, her heart cried out. *This way is better for you, my darlings. This way you will believe that at least I'm alive somewhere, that there's a possibility that one day I'll be found.* They wouldn't be left entirely without hope—as she was finally feeling herself to be.

She clenched the tiny bit of nail in her hand. It would have to do. She had nothing else to help pull her into 1777.

She removed all her clothing. Nothing she was wearing was appropriate. She'd make up excuses afterward. She should have considered this glitch, but now there was no time left.

Nude, she stepped out through the screen door, simultaneously viewing a team of snorting, straining horses drawing a rumbling cannon toward the house and Bob's unexpected car nearing the driveway. Why had he come home early today of all days? The sight of him nearly caused her to faint. Not now, she whispered fiercely, disciplining her mind to stay alert. He must not see her!

She ducked behind a small tree and some shrubs. It wasn't much of a hiding place, but she hadn't had time to run farther. The beagles were lying on the porch in the sunlight. Good dogs. Batty dogs, but good dogs. She'd miss them. She'd miss her children and her home and was sick with sadness. But she believed with deep conviction that she had done her best, her very, very best.

Bob pulled up to the house and got out of the car. Herkimer was yelling out orders in a deep, authoritative voice. "You better move fast or I'll skin you. Bring the cannon round, lads. Go for the base of the house. That'll be where the devils stowed the arms."

"General, sir, Bellwether's wife might be in there. We should check first, General." A young, beardless soldier stood at attention. He was wearing a tricorn hat, a blue coat with buff-colored cuffs and lapels, baggy leggings of brown linen and tall black boots with pewter buckles. Sweat rolled off his face; his clothing was soiled and torn. The day was a blistering one, the temperature nearing one hundred degrees.

Herkimer barked another order; several men cautiously entered the house. They soon emerged. "She's gone, General. And so's Enos." Likely, that explained why there had been no further recordings of the Bellwether's family tree, beyond Enos himself, in Grandma's Bible. He had been a turncoat.

"Then blow the bloody place to hell. And watch out for sparks blowing around. We don't need the woods going up in flames."

Bob walked inside calling for her. As he did, a terrible explosion blasted the building into complete shambles. For good measure, it was bombarded again. Debris flew skyward and sideward. Shards of glass and splintering lumber flew everywhere. The foundation crumbled and with it, the house. It collapsed in on itself with a terrible roar. The cannon boomed again, splintering the wreckage into yet smaller parts.

Jumping violently with each new eruption, Eloise remained crouched behind the foliage during the devastation. At last, silence and thick dust descended over the area. Black smoke billowed upward as the demolished building continued to burn. More explosions emitted from the cellar where apparently gunpowder had also been stored.

Finally it was over. She looked for Bob. Of course he wasn't to be seen. Neither was his car—or her world.

She blinked; the house was beginning to materialize. There was Bob standing on the porch, calling her name, looking around for her. The beagles were watching him, their ears alert. Only vaguely could she see the destroyed house. To her left, General Herkimer was fading and so were his men.

"No," she cried. "No." She hadn't made it, hadn't reached Marian. She hadn't thought things through enough. She was still *here*. Bob could see her. He had always been able to see her—her making love to Marian, her walking around the town at night. He probably saw her petting the town dogs, which to him would have been petting air. She had *failed*! She would never be able to permanently join Marian, her soul mate, her reason for living, for breathing, for *being*!

Eloise had also misjudged her shelter terribly. She hadn't managed to get nearly far enough away from flying debris as the house blew apart. First she was there and then she lay in a thousand pieces all over the ground. First there had been life; now there was nothing. She would never know the consequence of all her careful planning, would never know if she had been correct or not.

In a millisecond, it had all come undone.

Chapter Twenty-One

"Oh dear, oh dear, oh dear." Marian repeated the phrase over and over until it became a whisper and then only her lips moved as if in silent prayer as she ran to where Eloise lay and then knelt beside her.

Agnes was tight on her heels. "Why, Eloise is naked as a jaybird! Is she dead? She's dead, isn't she? I know it. I just *know* it?" She was becoming hysterical.

"Quiet, sister!" Marian shouted at her. Eloise moaned, heard a noise, didn't recognize it.

"Down!" Marian shouted. Both sisters fell across Eloise's body to protect it from another explosion. Another cannonball flew overhead. It overshot the remains of the house, landing with a thud and causing no damage as it exploded.

"Quick, help me lift her." Eloise heard Bob's voice. He had found her after all. Strangely, his masculine sounds blended into Marian's

172

anxious words. "I'll get you to a good doctor," they said. "The best there is."

"We've got to get away from here." Now she heard only Marian's voice, desperate and shaking as Agnes began to whimper. "Take hold, I say!" Alone, Marian lifted Eloise in her arms, grunting from the effort to stand. Agnes was obviously too stunned to move. "*Help* me, Agnes." Her sister blinked as though waking from a nightmare and grabbed the lower half of Eloise's body. They managed to carry her away from the noise and cannonballs still dropping around them.

"Can't they see us?" Agnes asked, grunting beneath the strain of half running, half walking toward Tomstown.

"Don't talk, just move," Marian admonished in a breathless voice. "This is no picnic we're on." Sweat flowed down her face. Agnes too, was saturated with perspiration.

"Why's she naked?" Agnes asked.

Eloise heard the question, but no answer. She hurt so, felt so sick that she didn't care that she was nude. She was heavily jostled as she was taken away. She fought to remember what had happened. There was an explosion, she knew that much. Oh, yes. Herkimer. Her head was now aching, her ears ringing. She could vaguely remember Bob—was his name Bob?—carrying her off.

People milled about. She heard Marian's voice shooing them off. Townspeople. Of course, they had also heard the bombing of her house and had come to see. The noise faded as she was placed onto something scratchy, a woolen blanket perhaps. Another was laid across her body and a cool cloth set upon her forehead. She tried to open her eyes, but it was too much effort. The women were talking and scurrying around the kitchen. She felt, rather than saw, Marian hovering about making her comfortable. At the sink, Agnes was pumping water into a bucket. Now she was stuffing wood into the firebox. There was noise, like that of war movies she had watched on . . . on . . . What was that thing called?

She opened her eyes and found herself wrapped in a blanket on the kitchen floor. Marian, leaning over her, replaced the cloth with a fresh one. "Oh, thank goodness," Marian exclaimed as soon as she saw Eloise's eyes focusing upon her. "How do you feel?" Eloise's lips were dry, her tongue too thick with dust to speak. "Here, drink a little water." Marian lifted her head to help her. She managed a sip or two.

"I knew General Herkimer was going to blow up that house," Eloise said in a hoarse whisper.

"No, dear, you couldn't have known," Marian said, brushing Eloise's damp hair from her brow. "Nobody knew except the men involved. It was all a secret, you see. We saw them coming down the road and ran to warn you, but—"

"No," Eloise protested. "I knew." She started to sit up, but Marian gently pushed her down. "I . . . I . . ."

"You've had a bad blow to your head, I think," Marian said gently, patting Eloise's face with the cloth.

"Of course," Eloise said. Now she remembered. Enos, finally having gone completely insane with jealousy, had taken away her clothing so that she couldn't go outdoors except to the backhouse, and on the way she had spotted Herkimer's troops. No, that wasn't true. A surge of fear washed over her. She was also going mad. She had children, Enos, a home. She fought off Marian as she struggled to sit up, dragging the blanket with her. She put her hand on Marian's shoulder to steady herself. "I've got children, Marian. I've got . . ." Her memory faded again as she lay back down.

"You have no children, Eloise."

"No children?" How could that be? They seemed so real to her. A boy and . . . a girl.

"None, Eloise, but . . ."

Eloise looked at her. "What?"

"You don't know?"

"Know what?"

"You're with child."

"No!"

Marian smiled. "Yes."

"How do you know?"

"Some things I just know. But Agnes is the one who keeps the family Bible, so she'll be writing in there when you were born, too, and your baby was born."

"I'm just nosy, that's all," Agnes said, smiling. She left the stove to sit near Eloise.

The air was slightly tinged with the smell of smoke. And there was baking bread, too. Eloise could smell that most strongly. Men were running around Tomstown bawling out orders, reorganizing, getting ready to return to their march. Piercing fife music was being played. No, it was a siren she was hearing. She immediately forgot the word *siren* and knew with certainty that she was listening to the high, sparkling tones of a fife. Thankfully, the explosions had ceased.

"I'll tell you plain, Eloise," Agnes explained matter-of-factly. "Sister can tell the future. She was born with a veil over her face."

Eloise had heard of people born with "veils," or cauls, over their faces. They were seers, foretellers of the future, could find dead people. Was Marian a witch? She shivered even though she still clung to the warm blanket.

"What's going to happen to me now, Marian? I'm homeless. The town will think me dreadful. And . . . where is Enos?" She sobbed, throwing an arm across her brow. "You tell me I'm with child. What am I to do now?" Sorrow overwhelmed her, her chest filling with it, oppressively bearing her down. She was leaving something very near and dear behind, and she couldn't remember it, not any of it.

Marian placed a kind hand on Eloise's shoulder. She spoke compassionately, her eyes filling with tears. "The town won't think you dreadful, my love. They know Enos's ways, and they know you as a good woman married to a bad man. And my guess, dear, is that he won't be back. He can't afford to. He's a turncoat. They'll hang him or shoot him on sight for that."

"Marian!" Agnes admonished.

"It's all right, Agnes," Eloise whispered. "I knew what would happen if he kept up his traitorous ways." How *did* she know that?

"You're going to be fine, Eloise," Marian said, patting her hand. Her flesh felt coarse and strong. A ripple of safety flowed through Eloise. "You'll live here with us, of course, and your child will be born here," Marian continued. "We'll all work together, love one another. We'll all be sisters instead of cousins. Maybe you can help teach the children to read, too."

"Well, we are all cousins, after all," Agnes added.

Yes, Eloise remembered that. They had talked about it last week when she had sneaked out of the house and gone blackberry-picking. No, that wasn't true . . . was it? Her head ached fiercely, and she closed her eyes.

Marian held Eloise's hand. "It's going to be very, very good, Eloise. Better than you can ever imagine—loved as you are." Eloise understood Marian's words as she added, "Sister and I will take you upstairs in a few minutes. First you must rest and get over your shock."

Eloise thought of Enos and how hard he had always been on her, how he had beaten her and denied her even the smallest comforts, like a few yards of new cloth or a second helping of blood pudding. Now he was gone from her life. In his place was Marian and Agnes—but mainly Marian. They had made love one time. One wonderful time.

Everything was quiet in the house, so quiet that she could hear King George purring. She wondered, did he ever leave his post?

Agnes settled at the table, while Marian remained seated beside Eloise, her hands, the hands that had so lovingly caressed her body and would again, she knew, lay primly folded and resting in her lap.

Eloise closed her eyes and slept.

ABOUT THE AUTHOR

Penny Hayes was born in Johnson City, NY on February 10, 1940. As a child she lived on a farm near Binghamton, NY. She later went to school in Utica and Buffalo, graduating with degrees in art, special education, elementary education and early childhood. Once a teacher in New York State and West Virginia, she is now retired and spends her time going on canoeing trips in Canada and New York, hiking New York and Vermont's trails and yearly participating in a cattle drive in Nevada for the Reno Rodeo. She is considering trying her hand at ranching for a week or two in New Mexico.

She presently lives between Monticello, NY and Ithaca, NY. She has two dogs, Ira and Buddy, who keep her as busy as any two-year-old child might.

Publications from
BELLA BOOKS, INC.
The best in contemporary lesbian fiction

P.O. Box 10543, Tallahassee, FL 32302
Phone: 800-729-4992
www.bellabooks.com

SUBSTITUTE FOR LOVE by Karin Kallmaker. One look and a deep kiss... Holly is hopelessly in lust. Can there be anything more?   ISBN 1-931513-62-7 $12.95

MAKING UP FOR LOST TIME by Karin Kallmaker. 240 pp. When three love-starved lesbians decide to make up for lost time, the recipe is romance.   ISBN 1-931513-61-9 $12.95

NEVER SAY NEVER by Linda Hill. 224 pp. A classic love story... where rules aren't the only things broken.   ISBN 1-931513-67-8 $12.95

PAINTED MOON by Karin Kallmaker. 214 pp. A snowbound weekend in a cabin brings Jackie and Leah together... or does it tear them apart?   ISBN 1-931513-53-8 $12.95

THE WAY LIFE SHOULD BE by Diana Tremain Braund. 173 pp. With which woman will Jennifer find the true meaning of love?   ISBN 1-931513-66-X $12.95

GULF BREEZE by Gerri Hill. Could Carly really be the woman Pat has always been searching for?   ISBN 1-931513-97-X $12.95

THE TOMSTOWN INCIDENT by Penny Hayes. 184 pp. Caught between two worlds, Eloise must make a decision that will change her life forever.   ISBN 1-931513-56-2 $12.95

BACK TO BASICS: A BUTCH/FEMME EROTIC JOURNEY edited by Therese Szymanski—from Bella After Dark. 324 pp.   ISBN 1-931513-35-X $12.95

SURVIVAL OF LOVE by Frankie J. Jones. 236 pp. What will Jody do when she falls in love with her best friend's daughter?   ISBN 1-931513-55-4 $12.95

DEATH BY DEATH by Claire McNab. 167 pp. 5th Denise Cleever Thriller.
   ISBN 1-931513-34-1 $12.95

CAUGHT IN THE NET by Jessica Thomas. 188 pp. A wickedly observant story of mystery, danger, and love in Provincetown.   ISBN 1-931513-54-6 $12.95

DREAMS FOUND by Lyn Denison. Australian Riley embarks on a journey to meet her birth mother . . . and gains not just a family, but the love of her life.   ISBN 1-931513-58-9 $12.95

A MOMENT'S INDISCRETION by Peggy J. Herring. 154 pp. Jackie is torn between her better judgment and the overwhelming attraction she feels for Valerie.
   ISBN 1-931513-59-7 $12.95